HE ESCORTED SUSANNA DOWN THE WHARF WITH GREAT
CEREMONY (*page* 80)

Susanna and Tristram

BY

MARJORIE HILL ALLEE

WITH ILLUSTRATIONS BY

HATTIE LONGSTREET PRICE

Boston and New York
HOUGHTON MIFFLIN COMPANY
The Riverside Press Cambridge

EIGHTEENTH PRINTING   R

The Riverside Press
CAMBRIDGE · MASSACHUSETTS
PRINTED IN THE U.S.A.

CONTENTS

ILLUSTRATIONS

SUSANNA AND TRISTRAM

• •

CHAPTER I

Susanna and Tristram Come to Town and Get a New Name

THE sun was bright, that March morning in the
early fifties, but the winds blowing down the Cincinnati hills were still cold. The President of the
Underground Railway buttoned his straight-collared Quaker coat a little higher as he paused on the
top step of his piazza and looked around him with
keen dark eyes.

He might have been thinking, like many other
good citizens of Cincinnati, that there was promise
of rain to raise the already dangerous level of the
great Ohio River. He might have been wondering
which of the muddy roads leading north from the
city offered the quickest and safest route for the
mysterious passengers of the Underground Railway. Or it might have been that he was only decid-
ing whether the latest free-labor calicoes that had
just reached his store from Philadelphia could be
sold at any profit. These prints were often coarse
cloth, and of little variety, and he himself loved
good materials so well that he could understand the

Cincinnati women who wanted better, even if it were made from cotton grown by slave labor. He might have to ship these bolts of cloth up to some Indiana country store before they could be sold at all.

Whatever his thoughts, they did not change by so much as a ripple the kind, meditative expression on his clean-shaven face. It was only when his attention was caught by a horse and rider halting in front of his house that his eyes narrowed with interest and he swung down the steps quickly and quietly.

On a broad-backed old white horse, whose legs were caked with mud, sat a big girl, steadily regarding him with eyes as piercing as his own. A bag thrown across behind the saddle served as pillion for a small boy, who clung to the girl and peeped out from behind her shoulder with the shyness of a country child among strangers.

Much experience had prepared Levi Coffin for unannounced visitors of a sort, but not for these. This flaxen-haired pair would not want transportation over the Underground Railway, but they looked shabby enough to need almost anything else.

'Well, friend,' he said courteously to the big girl, who had not spoken, 'what can I do for thee?'

The girl swallowed hard; she was almost as frightened as the little boy, but she must not show it.

'I'm Susanna Coffin,' she said at last, in a drawl that Levi Coffin, who was himself Southern bred, recognized as partly her own and partly Carolinian. 'This here is Tristram, my little brother.' The affection in her voice was like a reassuring touch of the hand to little scared Tristram.

The man's face lighted.

'I take it thou art from the Nantucket Coffin stock, though I can't name thy branch of the family yet. Both of you have the square Coffin chin. Will you alight and make us a visit? Katy will be glad to see you both. How did thee happen to find us?'

Tristram stirred at once, ready to turn on his stomach and slide down from his tiring perch, but Susanna sat still, firmly fixed in her battered saddle. She had not finished introducing herself.

'Cousin Folger Coffin sent us,' she went on.

'Folger? Has thee come from Indiana? I judged thee was from the North State.'

'I did come from North Car'linya. Two years ago, it was. Father and Mother and the two boys all died with the fever. We hadn't any nearer kin than Cousin Folger, so the neighbors allowed Tristram and I had better go out to Indiana. There was a wagon traveling through that we could follow. So we did.

'This winter Cousin Folger got thy letter asking for one of his boys to help keep store. He said he was going to need all the boys to plow this spring, and so he sent Tristram and me down instead.

'Cousin Folger hasn't got on very well,' she added impartially. 'He's always having bad luck with his stock, or the frost kills the corn. Or something. But this year they hadn't had so much chills and fever, and Folger was counting on the boys to put him in a big corn crop and maybe make some money. He said to tell thee that.'

'I know Folger Coffin,' the other said dryly. 'If he were not a Coffin I'd be tempted to call him poor white trash; but I did think that some of his boys might show the good stock they come from. And I needed help, though not for store-keeping. That must have been Folger's own idea.

'Well, get down, get down! We'll be glad to see what we can do for thee. Thee seems to be much alone in the world.'

To his surprise the girl still sat stubbornly where she was, her cheeks a little more flushed.

'Tristram and I have spent nearly two years where they didn't want us and said they didn't need us. I don't intend to impose on anybody again, even if their name is Coffin! If thee can give me some work where I can earn board and keep for us, I'll take it and thank thee. I'm strong. I can make as good a hand in the field as any of Folger Coffin's boys; and Mother taught me how to cook and sew and spin. And I'm good at figures, too.

THE OLD WHITE HORSE RELUCTANTLY CONSENTED TO TURN
AND FOLLOW HIM

That was why I thought I might be able to help in the store as well as a boy. But maybe ——' she looked down at her square weather-beaten hands and faded old riding-skirt — 'maybe I wouldn't do for that. In a fine city like Cincinnati. But I can do something!'

Levi Coffin was smiling now.

'Well, well,' he said, 'I like thy spirit, and I think I know the place for thee. Katy and I would have been glad to have a visit from you two, but I can see thee will feel easier to be independent. I am going over to the store now. Thee can ride along and wait for me and then I shall be free to see to thee.' Without further explanation he set off up the street.

The old white horse reluctantly consented to turn and follow him. The hilly approach to Cincinnati had strained her tired legs, and she did not want to move at all, particularly into the noisy city traffic, clattering by over cobblestones. Susanna had her hands full quieting Whitey, who shied like a silly colt, and seeing that the excited Tristram did not dislodge either himself or her from the side-saddle.

'Thee said Cousin Levi Coffin was President of the Underground Railway, didn't thee?' Tristram demanded. 'Is he going to the station now? How does it go underground? Can I ride on it, 'Sanna?'

'Tristram! Doesn't thee really know any better

than that? There isn't any real railway at all. The people who help slaves to escape were so clever and quiet about it that somebody said once they must have an underground railway to send them on; and they said Levi Coffin must be the president of it, because he helped more slaves than anybody else. It was just a joke.'

'I hoped I could ride on it,' said the little boy sadly. 'I never did ride on a railway. Is thee sure, 'Sanna?'

'I'll take thee for a railway ride some day, Brother, when I'm very old and rich. I don't think thee'd like the Underground. They say that Underground passengers have to travel at night and hide in the daytime.

'Watch out, Tristram! That boy is throwing a rock!'

Susanna had seen that the figure of their guide attracted considerable attention. Nearly every one he met threw him a glance of recognition and he spoke gravely to all. Some smiled and bowed, a few fairly scowled at him; just now a small boy, about five years old, not yet out of dresses, scrabbled around until he found a pebble he could manage to throw.

This he flung with great energy, evidently intending it for the back of the President of the Underground Railway, striding on ahead of him, but the hold of his fat fingers was uncertain, the stone slipped and sailed away on a tangent behind him, striking old Whitey's foreleg and causing her to shy dangerously, as much from surprise as from hurt.

The small boy never saw what had happened. As soon as the stone left his hand, he had dodged to shelter behind a newly leafing lilac bush, calling from this screen, 'Nigger-stealer! Nigger-stealer!' And from thence he thought it best to run for his own back door.

In those days there was more than one person who suspected Levi Coffin of mysterious powers that ordinary human beings did not own. Now he gave fresh proof of them. He had not turned around nor even wavered in his steady course; Susanna would not have said that he noticed when the startled Whitey had nearly unseated her. Nevertheless, she saw him stop squarely before a young man whom he met a block or so farther on, and heard a surprising conversation as she waited.

The young man replied politely but uneasily to the greeting of the elder. It was plain that he would have preferred avoiding any talk, but Levi Coffin had no intention of letting him off.

'I have had it in mind for the last week to speak to thee about the bill thee is owing at the store,' he said directly. 'Thee knows the free-labor associations run on a small capital, and we must keep that clear so far as possible to buy new stocks of goods when the old are sold out. Can thee let me have the money by the first of the month?'

The young man looked more uneasy than ever. 'I — I don't see how I can,' he stammered. 'I can pay something, of course, but I'd counted on letting that bill run till May.'

Levi Coffin shook his head with grave disapproval. 'My dear young friend,' he said, 'I am afraid thee isn't keeping thy business well in hand at home or abroad. When I went past thy house just now thy little Johnny called me "Nigger-stealer" and threw a stone that struck the horse of my young friends here.

'Now thy father was a sound business man and held his family to high principles. He was no slavery man, nor did he bring up his sons to be.'

'He hadn't married a wife from Kentucky,' the young man answered miserably. 'I do the best I can with Caroline. I don't let her bring any slaves up here, and I have her trade at your free-labor store, though I can tell you she don't like it; and I try to keep her from putting ideas into the boy's head. Fact is, he gets that rough talk from the other children. When you're just across the river from a slave State, it's mighty hard to keep separate.'

The older man was watching his face closely.

'I will see what I can do personally about thy bill,' he said. 'Perhaps we can let it run a little longer.

'But another matter. Wouldn't thee like to take

a few shares in the Underground Railway? The treasury is a little low, and I feel certain passengers will continue to come. Even if thee can't pay out now on thy store bill, thee might be able to spare a dollar or two for my other business.'

'Guess I can't do anything less,' answered the young man, hunting out a worn bill from his pocket and handing it over with a wry grin. 'I understand this makes me liable to arrest for aiding slaves to escape?'

'I understand so,' the other replied placidly. 'Though I never have known of any such arrest among our subscribers. And many have told me that they were very well satisfied with the investment, and gave me more.'

With something very like a twinkle in his eye he went on. Here was one man who would not make trouble for the Underground, no matter what his neighbors or his Southern wife might urge. Even if he forgot his debt to the store, and Levi Coffin did not intend to let him forget it, he would still be afraid of being reported as himself a subscriber to the Railway.

Outside the plain store Susanna sat in her saddle and wondered what would come next. Through all the week that it had taken her to ride down from central Indiana she had not found it so hard to wait as she had for the last hour. Tristram slid down and walked timidly up the street to see the near-by amazing sights of a city of more than a hundred thousand people. There were four-story and even five-story buildings, with tall windows where many things were temptingly displayed to the country boy's eyes. When he reported finding stick candy in one, Susanna became extravagant and gave him one of her few pennies to buy some.

Tristram sat then on the edge of a stone doorstep and ate a red-striped stick as slowly as possible, watching the people go by until his eyes and neck-bones were tired of turning like an owl's. Every one seemed to him very stylishly dressed, but it did not occur to him that he looked odd in his home-spun, home-woven, home-made suit of plain Quaker cut, until three boys, all a little larger than Tristram, stopped in front of him and began to nudge each other and snicker.

Left alone, Tristram would probably have honestly admired their frilled shirts and silk neckties, the like of which he never expected to have for himself; but under their stares he decided promptly that he did not care for them at all, in any way, and started for Susanna.

One youngster put out a practiced foot, over which Tristram stumbled and dropped his precious candy in recovering his balance. He was afraid to stop for the candy; he ran on down the street, and the three boys, much encouraged, followed, shrieking, 'Quaker! Qua-ker!'

One of them so nearly caught up with Tristram that he undertook a kick at the country boy's flying heels. It was not a well-judged kick. Susanna had the satisfaction of seeing the kicker miss Tristram altogether and sit down heavily in a puddle, while the other boys charged on, not prepared to see Tristram stop suddenly by old Whitey and swarm up to his pillion seat.

''Sanna, I lost my candy,' he sobbed breathlessly. 'Can't we ride up and get it? I could wash it off.'

'No,' said his sister firmly. 'I never saw such a dirty place. It looks like there had been droves of pigs all along these streets, and people just as piggy. When I can spare another penny I'll give it to thee, Brother; or maybe we can find some fresh tree-sugar. I like that better.'

'I don't,' said Tristram mournfully.

The three boys had planted themselves across the street safely out of reach of Susanna, who looked too big and strong for close range, and when there were not too many passers-by they called 'Quaker!' again, or 'Thee little thee!' in high, squeaking tones with much giggling.

'Wish I had something to throw at them!' Tristram muttered.

'They're worse off than thee is,' Susanna reminded him. 'Look at the mud on the fine green trousers of that fat boy!'

'Calling us names!' growled Tristram.

'Well, isn't thee a Quaker?' his sister asked reasonably. 'And thee knows very well that Quakers don't quarrel or fight. That only makes more trouble.'

Tristram sighed and was quiet. He was very glad when Levi Coffin appeared at the door and stood there a moment gazing across the street. The three boys fled from that clear gaze, as if he had been the Recording Angel, writing down their naughty deeds to remember for judgment.

'Can thee take this bundle conveniently?' he asked Susanna then. 'We go on up the hill now. Does thee mind the grade? I rode out from Carolina to Indiana myself, when I was not much older than thee, and I always found upgrade easier than downhill.'

They set off again to the northeast. Levi Coffin's home was well downtown, not a great distance from the river, in the older settled part of the city. As they went along now, they came gradually into a section where groups of houses were separated by fields that had not been divided into city lots at all. After a time they turned into a street that was little more than a country road, with houses set fairly close together. Each had its big garden and fruit trees, its small barn and chicken-house. Tristram began to feel more cheerful. He had seen small reason that morning for liking the city, but he knew the country and felt more at home here.

By a white-painted gate Levi Coffin stopped and looked up at Susanna with a half smile, as if he kept a little joke to himself.

'This is the place I have in mind for thee,' he said. 'A German couple that I know live here. The husband runs a livery stable downtown and his business is growing so that he hasn't time to work around home.

'His wife asked me to find a good strong girl to stay with her. She said she did not want a boy, because boys were not neat. I told her there was not a girl of the kind she wanted nearer than Germany, but when I saw thee this morning I decided I might have been mistaken.'

Susanna slid down from her horse, as she saw she was expected to do.

'I never did see a German,' she said slowly, unfastening the black calico riding-skirt that had protected her plain shabby dress.

'These are good people,' Levi Coffin assured her. 'I trust them.'

She was to learn later that this was high praise.

'That bundle I gave thee,' he added, seeing that she hardly knew what to do with it, 'has a dress and a bonnet in it that may fit thee. My Katy and her sewing circle keep me supplied with clothes that passengers on the Underground Railway may need, and I thought thee might find these of use in thy present position. No, thee doesn't owe me thanks.'

Susanna flushed with embarrassment.

'I do thank thee,' she said as she knotted Whitey's rein securely to the hitching-post, but any other expression of gratitude was driven from her head by Cousin Levi's next speech, by far the most unexpected feature of an unusual morning.

'I think it might be best for thee, while thee is living here, to go by the name of this family, instead of our own,' he said, as serenely as if he were advising her to wear brown instead of gray.

Susanna turned astonished blue eyes to him. He was not a tall man. The girl herself was fully his height. Nor was he imposing in dress or appearance. The tone was kind, the ageing face was kind, but there was nevertheless so much authority in both that Susanna did not dare make her protest.

'I should like thee to take my judgment in this,' he went on. 'I believe thee can be a help to me, if thee can carry out my directions.'

'Wh-what is the name?' stammered Susanna.

The little smile came back faintly as he took her shapeless bag from behind the saddle and ushered her up the neat path.

'Rammelsberg is the name.'

'What did thee say?'

'Rammelsberg,' repeated Levi Coffin slowly and patiently.

'Susanna Rammelsberg,' said his young cousin, with no liking for the combination. 'Must Tristram be German, too?'

'I think it would be wiser.'

Tristram, unconsulted, wailed, 'It's worse than Coffin, and I used to think that was the ugliest name any boy could have!'

'S-sh, Brother!' Susanna cautioned hastily, for the shining knob of the front door was opening and a hearty voice called, 'Vell, vell, come in yet!'

The next minute Susanna and Tristram Coffin were being received into the Rammelsberg house.

CHAPTER II

Susanna Meets Jack Fairfield

SUSANNA and Tristram stood at one side of Mrs. Rammelsberg's front hall waiting for Levi Coffin to finish explaining about them and Mrs. Rammelsberg to finish understanding about them. Of Mrs. Rammelsberg's German-flavored English they understood not more than two words in ten; and Cousin Levi's voice was so low that they could not catch what he said, even when they were impolite enough to try. They only knew that at the end of ten or fifteen minutes, everything seemed to have been settled satisfactorily between the two older people, and Levi Coffin bade them a kindly good-bye and hurried off.

'He is a goot man,' said Mrs. Rammelsberg heartily, watching him off down the path. '*Himmel!* How much goot that man does! Is that your own horse, my Susanna? Mr. Coffin does not seem to take it. Vell, vell, you must see to it later. Now I vill show you vere you are to stay.'

She launched herself briskly at the first step of the stairway, paused, looked around at the shabby pair, and proceeded a little less determinedly.

The bedroom that she showed them was spotless and unwrinkled beyond anything that either Susanna or Tristram had ever encountered. The feather bed, covered with a hand-woven spread of elaborate design, puffed up like a loaf of bread ready for the baking. The crocheted tidies on the chair backs and the lace-edged curtains fairly shouted that they were fresh from the washtub and iron. Even the rag carpet on the floor was so bright and unused that Susanna hesitated to set down her mud-spattered baggage.

Mrs. Rammelsberg noticed her hesitation and her face glowed again.

'You have right, my Susanna, you have right! This is not the place for a fine little boy like your brother. Vat is it that you call him? Tr-ristr-ram? That vill never do! Never can I say those "r-r's" so many times a day as one must call after a little boy. Hans, now; that is a fine name for a boy. Yes? Let us call him Hans!'

Tristram gazed at her in wordless dismay; to find himself in half an hour become Hans Rammelsberg instead of Tristram Coffin was like a bad dream. He did not know what might happen to him next. He clung to his sister's strong, warm hand and found himself hurrying downstairs again, after Mrs. Rammelsberg, who talked all the way.

The house looked modest enough from the road, but it extended back a surprising distance. Through the chilly front hall, back through a spick-and-span sitting-room without a sign of fire in its polished stove, and into a gleaming kitchen they followed. Here there was no fire either, but Mrs. Rammelsberg could not forbear pausing a moment to cast a glance of pride over her shelves of shining brass and well-scoured pewter.

'My new stove,' she pointed out. 'Is it not goot? Made here in the city.'

Susanna regarded it with professional interest.

'I've seen a stove,' she said, 'but I've never cooked on one. Do you have a fireplace, too?'

The woman looked at her sharply.

'From the country you are. Yes, of course; Mr. Coffin say from the South. I hear they cook very goot in the South. Now, this new stove I do not use, but I have another, older, in the kitchen yet, that cooks fine. You vill learn a stove. It is not hard.'

She bustled on again.

'Come. This little stairs takes us up to a room you vill like, over my kitchen with the warm stove. The stovepipe comes up through the room and heats it. See a little bed for you here, and over there another little bed for your brother. Do you not like it?'

She beamed at them happily, evidently much better pleased with an arrangement that spared her fine bedroom. Susanna and Tristram felt much more at home, too, in this long loft with the sloping roof. There were red-and-black homespun blankets

'COME. THIS LITTLE STAIRS TAKES US UP TO A ROOM YOU
VILL LIKE'

on the narrow beds, and patchwork quilts, not too fine for use, to cover them. The drum in the stove-pipe gave out a comforting warmth, and Mrs. Rammelsberg patted it lovingly before she left them.

'Come down ven you have unpacked,' she told them. 'Then you must see to that poor dirty horse, and it vill be time for our dinner already.'

Mrs. Rammelsberg's cookery was strange to them, but very good. The two fell on the German food with appetites that delighted the good woman, herself as round and rosy as if she found it very nourishing. Since a cold and scanty breakfast at four o'clock they had had neither food nor rest, and Susanna was not surprised to see Tristram's fair head nod and rest on the red tablecloth beside the plate that held the last crumbs of his coffee cake.

'Such a fine boy,' commented Mrs. Rammels-berg comfortably. 'So blond he might be German himself. And you, too; yes? Maybe you could carry him up to his bed and let him sleep. I do not often like boys; they are too dirty and careless; but this little one, he reminds me of my brother in the old country. I shall like to call him Hans, too; that was my brother's name.'

Susanna felt very much the better for her good dinner, and grateful to Mrs. Rammelsberg for food and shelter and warmth. All the afternoon she worked, under a continuous stream of direction.

She was awkward, but willing, and her strength pleased her new employer.

'These American girls, they are not much goot, *nein!*' she commented. 'But you have been better brought up. I can see that ve shall plow the garden, even, this spring, vithout troubling the mister.

'And you like animals, is it not so? For I see that they like you. You feed the chickens vithout scaring them, and your poor old horse you made clean and comfortable before you vere fed yourself. I think Mr. Coffin vas kind to me ven he brought you here!'

She put her hands on her hips and faced Susanna seriously, tilting her face up to look into the girl's eyes.

'Mr. Coffin tells me it vas better you should be Rammelsberg vile you are here by us. You understand that, too? I think you could maybe be my niece so vell as anything.

'All men are brothers, Mr. Coffin says; but after that ve can decide for ourselves, *hein?* So I vill decide for you to be my niece and I vill be your aunt, and the little Hans, your brother, he is of course my nephew. Though by marriage, of course. Ve must not forget that. You vill be a daughter of my Anton's sister that died in the east. It vas the east of Berlin, but ve vill not tell that. Ve vill not talk much about it at all. Yes?'

'I don't talk much,' answered Susanna soberly.

'And I believe you there,' returned Mrs. Rammelsberg. 'Now let us go dig up some apples in the garden. Did you never hear of that? In the fall ve dig a hole and put apples in it covered vith straw; then ve cover it vith earth and leave all vinter, and in the spring they are dug up again and ve make apfel-strudel. Hans, he vill like apfel-strudel for his supper. I show you how to make it!'

The newly adopted niece went to bed very early that night, so tired that she fell asleep in the middle of Tristram's questions and confidences. Some time later she wakened at a new noise that floated up to her little window under the eaves.

It seemed as if she had been asleep for a very long time, but it could not have been very late, for presently she collected her sleepy wits enough to make out that Mr. Rammelsberg had come home from the livery stable and was being made fit to enter the house. Susanna had not yet seen him. Mrs. Rammelsberg had said that he had not time to climb the hill for his dinner, and so took with him in the morning a cold lunch and a pail of coffee to warm on the stable stove.

Susanna suspected now, as she heard him shedding boots, coat, and hat at the chilly doorstep while his wife fetched slippers and a basin of hot soapsuds to the bench outside the door, that he really had not time at noon for the scrubbing that would be required of him. She was relieved when the bustle died down and the creak of a rocking-chair signaled up through the kitchen ceiling that Mr. Rammelsberg was resting with his clean feet warming at the oven of the second best cook-stove.

The girl's mind turned back to her own affairs. She and Tristram seemed to have reached a safe corner for a little while, even if it was a rather queer corner. She had set out with dread to hunt up Cousin Levi Coffin, but now it seemed to have been the best thing to do.

Two years before she had bundled up her little brother and started to Indiana with a brave heart. She was then barely fourteen, but she was big and strong, and all her life she had heard stories of neighbors and relatives who had gone West and prospered. It was true that except for Tristram she had no close relative in the world, and that she had only a small sum of money and the old white horse they rode on; but she had no doubt that she and her brother would grow up to take care of each other, and people had always been kind to them.

Since then she had usually been without comforts and often unhappy; worst of all, she had not always been able to take care of Tristram. He had been cold and badly fed; and Folger Coffin had taken her money to pay for their keep, so that she had found it hard to buy even the simplest clothes. She felt as if she had grown old in a great hurry those last two years.

She could not be sorry to leave Folger Coffin's slovenly log cabin, filled with quarreling children and surrounded by half-cleared fields where no crop ever looked well-grown; but she had been afraid of the city, too. Where could a country girl like herself find a place to fill in the greatest city west of the Allegheny Mountains? The fortune of the day had fallen out better than she could have hoped.

One thing was wrong. Why could she not be Susanna Coffin? She had never thought Coffin a handsome name, but for all that she would not have changed it for the oldest name in Virginia. It stood for a solid, well-known family tradition, stretching back through the first Tristram of Nantucket Island into Old England, where there were landed estates of knights of that name from the time of William the Conqueror. Even shiftless Folger Coffin knew that and was proud of it.

Susanna, poor child, could think of only one explanation for Levi Coffin's odd request. He must be ashamed of her. She knew that he was a man of means and position, in spite of the fact that many people hated him bitterly on account of his activities in helping escaped slaves on to Canada. He must not want to appear to be connected with his distant and poverty-stricken young cousins from the backwoods of North Carolina. Susanna had been made fun of more than once by Western people, whose own fathers had emigrated up from the North State in the earlier days and were rather ashamed of their origin.

The girl made up her mind that neither she nor Tristram would trouble him, if he felt so, and on that she went to sleep.

It was a stout resolution, but she was allowed to keep it only overnight. At sunrise Mrs. Rammelsberg's cheerful voice filled the steep stairway, "'Sanna! Su-sanna!'

Susanna sat up before she was really awake to hear the voice going on with instructions.

'Your good dress, Mr. Coffin gave you, you could put on right avay to run an errand for me. Let the little Hans sleep, if he vill. He can then be no trouble to me.'

'You look fine,' Mrs. Rammelsberg assured her later, looking her up and down, twitching the fitted bodice, arranging the gathers of the full skirt, and smoothing Susanna's straight fine hair down over her ears. 'Fine, but not too fine. I like Mr. Coffin's taste. He vas not made to be a Qvaker; he knows clothes too vell. I tell myself that he gets fun out of his railvay, dressing up his passengers. You vill see!'

The dark blue cloth dress, trimmed with a little velvet, was by far the best that Susanna's wardrobe had ever boasted. She had considered herself lucky if she had one unpatched woolen dress for winter,

and two cotton ones for summer. The bonnet that
went with the dress was a problem to her. Her
Quaker scoop bonnet, which had also been her
mother's, settled over her head like a sunbonnet,
but this trifle of shirred silk, with a wreath of flowers under the brim, was evidently not meant to
shade her face at all. Mrs. Rammelsberg settled
the question by putting it on the girl's head and
tying the wide satin ribbons under her square chin.

'It feels like it was slipping off the back of my
head,' Susanna protested.

'That is to show the hair. Your hair, it is pretty.
Yes!'

'I don't think so,' said Susanna honestly. 'When
I was a little girl I dipped my head into Mother's
indigo dyeing pot, because I hoped the yellow and
blue would go together and make my hair green!'

Mrs. Rammelsberg threw up her hands with
amusement and horror.

'You are a young lady now. You vill learn better. Even a Qvaker girl must some day find out
that she is beautiful!

'But, look, ve are late! Mrs. Coffin vill be saying,
"Vere are now the fresh eggs for breakfast?" Here
is the basket. You know the vay? I said to myself,
"That Susanna is a bright girl and she vill remember vat she has seen and heard." It is downhill
and not too far to valk for a strong girl like you.
If Mr. and Mrs. Coffin have errands for you, you

are to stay and do what they ask. Mr. Coffin arranged that yesterday. I vill take care of the little
boy.'

Susanna went along through the chill early morning with the basket of eggs on her arm, concerned
to keep her skirts and the shawl Mrs. Rammelsberg
had lent her from the damp grass and roadside
puddles. It had rained in the night while she slept,
and there was promise of more showers in the clouds
that had already hid the rising sun. It was very
odd, she thought, that she should be sent to the
Coffin house just as she had made up her mind that
Levi Coffin did not want to have anything more to
do with her. She wondered what errands Mrs.
Rammelsberg thought the Coffins might have for
her.

The Coffin house seemed to Susanna even larger
and more imposing than it had the day before. On
consideration she decided to take the eggs to the
door farthest back, and even here her heart
thumped as she waited. The kitchen door was
opened by a sweet-faced, white-capped woman,
who surveyed Susanna through her spectacles and
evidently recognized the dress and the girl at once.

'Thee bring the eggs right in,' she requested.
'Ellen was just ready to make her corn-bread. Will
thee sit down and rest and have a bite before thee
goes?'

Susanna would have preferred to go back to

Tristram, but she felt that perhaps Mrs. Rammelsberg's orders covered even this invitation. She sat
down shyly on the edge of a splint-bottomed chair
and waited, while the young colored girl at the
table mixed the batter for her corn-bread.

'You-all make your corn-bread with eggs?' she
ventured presently with real curiosity, for she was
already an experienced cook. 'We never did, back
home.'

The colored girl looked up at her with sharp fear
and fled without answering into the dining-room
after the older woman.

Susanna could hear her protesting, 'But I *know*
she's from the South. She talks that way.'

The two came back to the kitchen together,
where Susanna sat, surprised and apologetic.

'Ellen is nervous,' the older woman explained
quietly to Susanna. 'She is afraid thee isn't
friendly. Ellen, doesn't thee know thee will be
taken care of in this house? No harm has ever come
to one of thy people within our walls. Thy fear is
thy own worst enemy. It betrays thee.'

The girl went back to her cooking, wiping her
wet cheeks, but effectually calmed.

'Seems like I cain't help it,' she explained. 'I get
scared so easy I lose my sense. Mr. Coffin thinks I
better go on North where I feel safe, but I did want
to work for Mrs. Coffin awhile to pay a little for
what I owe them for helping me.'

She went on more cheerfully to exchange with Susanna recipes for corn-pone and beaten biscuit, but when a knock came at the kitchen door she dodged, as if from an expected blow, and edged back into a dim corner while the older woman answered the door, her quiet manner unruffled.

'Well, Aunt Katy,' Susanna heard a man's voice without, tired, but irrepressibly gay, 'the bad penny is back!'

'Who ——? Why, John Fairfield!' Catherine Coffin exclaimed. 'Dear friend, what has thee been doing? Come in before some one sees thee!'

The door frame was nearly filled with a tall young man, whose torn clothes had evidently been thoroughly drenched and since then had partially dried on him. His hands and face were streaked with brown mud that the same water might have left. Through this clown's mask of dirt his dark eyes flashed and his white teeth showed in a most engaging grin.

'Better put an old piece of carpet by the stove for me to stand on while I talk, Aunt Katy,' he said. 'I don't want to drip on your clean floor. You might not let me come again.'

'Thee knows better,' said Catherine Coffin, seeming with the same swift motion to usher him to a rocker close by the stove and find him a cup of hot coffee.

She opened then the door of a little back stairway

'WELL, AUNT KATY, THE BAD PENNY IS BACK!'

and said, without lifting her clear voice, 'Levi, can thee come here? I need thee!'

Levi Coffin looked quizzically at his bedraggled visitor.

'Well, Jack Fairfield, what can I do for thee this time, besides giving thee dry clothes?'

The young man rose respectfully, flashing the same delightful smile down from his considerable height.

'I will admit, suh, that dry clothes would make me less conspicuous on the streets of your metropolis; but I did not come for that. I must have help for my friends. I have got them into a bad place and can't get them out by myself.'

Levi Coffin shook his head. 'Into trouble again,' he rebuked the young man affectionately. 'Thy wild ways get the better of thee. Who are thy friends?'

Jack Fairfield spread his arms wide.

'All Kentucky, suh; all Kentucky! A case after your own heart, though you would never admit it.'

He laughed with enjoyment, and helped himself to a large piece of the admiring Ellen's hot corn·bread.

CHAPTER III

The Funeral Procession that was not What it Seemed

'ALL Kentucky ——' repeated Levi Coffin dryly. 'I have heard that before.'

'How many runaways were there, then?' asked Jack Fairfield, deftly abstracting a slice of crisp bacon from the hot platter on the stove beside him.

'Seventeen. That was when we lived back in Indiana.'

Jack Fairfield appeared to be calculating. 'There was twenty-eight nigroes in this bunch of mine when I counted them last down by Mill Crick; including a baby that *would* yell at the wrong time!'

'Twenty-eight? Does thee mean it?' Levi Coffin's tone lost its last trace of reproof. He was keenly interested. 'What has thee done with them? Tell us at once.'

Jack Fairfield flattened his long slim body against the warm wall by the stove.

'Well, suh,' he confided, 'I been buying poultry for the last few weeks across the river and down a little way. About twenty miles. I have not paid for any of it and I'm right afraid I never will. But then I never expect to get any of the chickens, either. When I was looking at their old hens, I was so pro-slavery that you'd be surprised; but that didn't bother the nigroes much.'

He smiled sweetly.

'Some of them had a little money they could give me, and I took it, though I knew you wouldn't approve, suh. I'm not an independent business man like you, and my Virginia folks would rather vote for Seward himself than give me a penny. They know me by this time. I've helped my own uncle's slaves escape. But you can see that if I go around buying poultry and organizing these little excursions for colored people, I need some money. Well, I don't apologize.

'This bunch of nigroes that wanted to get away with me kept getting more numerous; the men wanted to take their wives, and this one woman would take her baby. There were really too many.

'As soon as it was dark last night I took the whole kit and caboodle down to a woodyard across from the mouth of the Big Miami; I knew some skiffs were tied up there. The river is up so high that we didn't have to watch out as careful as sometimes. Nobody would be looking for runaway nigroes crossing as near flood as the river is now.

'I put them all on three big skiffs. It was too crowded; I was afraid we might get in each other's way if we took more, but we'd better have taken that risk. The boats were overloaded and shipped water, and mine leaked. It was about to sink before we reached the Ohio side. I jumped out on a sand-bar to see if I could pull it ashore, and then if I didn't get stuck in the mud! Some of the nigroes had to pull me loose. Every last one of us finally had to wade to shore, and some of them lost their poor old shoes in the mud. And how that baby did yell!'

He took another piece of corn-bread.

Levi Coffin said, 'Did thee buy the skiffs, or did some one give them to you?'

'I stole them,' Jack answered calmly.

'Thee saw no harm in that? Thee couldn't even return them.'

'Slaves are stolen property,' the young man returned, his dark eyes flashing. 'I can't see that it is any harm to steal boats or horses or anything else that will help give them their rightful freedom.'

Levi Coffin sighed. 'I fear trouble for thee,' he said.

'I *know* I'm going to get trouble,' Jack said confidently. 'All night I've had nothing but trouble, and it wasn't all leaky skiffs, either. I had to herd that crowd of nigroes up this way along shore; scold them and encourage them and tell them it was only a little farther along when I knew it was ten miles yet! Nothing but a little towpath to follow in the dark, and part of them without even any shoes. When that rain came up, they got too miserable to complain.

'I couldn't get them safe into town before daybreak, and after daylight the stupidest policeman in town would have arrested them on sight as fugitives.

'I found a nice slippery ravine or two down below Mill Crick, and left them there while I came on to see what could be done. I stopped at this colored preacher's, John Hatfield; but he didn't know how to plan any more than I did. So I came on over here, suh, knowing that under your calm and innocent exterior there lay a great gift for dramatics. What game is it that we shall play this time, suh?'

Levi Coffin frowned, though not from Fairfield's teasing.

'Twenty-eight people,' he said to himself. 'And all cold and wet and hungry. I could wish, John, that thee had restrained thyself to half the number.'

'We might bring them in two and three at a time,' suggested the young man, not very hopefully.

'No. It would take too long. They have suffered enough from exposure to need relief as soon as possible. But such a conspicuous number of them!'

'Could some one drive out with one of these covered mover's wagons?'

The older man shook his gray head. 'Too noticeable, even if we knew where to get one. Thee said they are out by Mill Creek?'

'Yes, suh.'

'I went up that Mill Creek road not long ago, past the colored burying-ground. I know it. Jack!' — the little twinkle shone in his keen eyes — 'I believe we had best have a funeral; a funeral procession, at least. No one will interfere with that no matter how many negroes there may be riding in it.'

'Suh,' said Jack admiringly, 'I knew I could depend on you. I am far from understanding the details, but lead on and I follow. The tale will be worth telling afterward.'

'I am inclined to think that thy part is done, Jack,' said Levi Coffin gently. 'Let Catherine provide thee with dry clothes and then take some rest. Thee is known here, and we may be safer without thy help.'

Jack's face fell.

'And so are you known here, suh, if I may suggest the fact. Why should I be out of the fun if you are in it?'

'I shan't appear in it directly. This young friend will go on some errands for me. Susanna!'

Susanna fairly jumped. She had been leaning forward in her chair, entirely absorbed in the story that was unfolding before her. She came over timidly to the group by the stove and stood there, suddenly the center of attention.

'John Fairfield,' said Levi Coffin, 'this young woman has only just come to Cincinnati. No one knows her in connection with the Underground Railway, and I feel we can trust her. Since she happens to be here this morning she can help us, if she will.'

Susanna, under the critical eyes of the young man, felt very young and gawky even in her prized new clothes.

'She looks trustworthy,' Jack admitted. 'A relative of yours, you say?'

Susanna flushed, but Levi Coffin answered calmly: 'I said she was a young friend, newly come to the city. She lives with Mrs. Rammelsberg, and I am going to send her now to the Rammelsberg livery stable with a message.

'Susanna, I will write thee a note to carry to Anton Rammelsberg. Hand it to him thyself and tell him there must be haste.'

'But, suh,' Jack caught him up, 'is a note safe? Not that I care a fig for personal danger, as you very well know, but it might, if found, make our future work in Cincinnati more difficult. I take any means, safe or risky, to get escaping slaves here, but I count on smooth sailing once they are here under your care.'

'This note will be safe enough,' Levi Coffin promised. 'Thee forgets I am an old hand at this business. I was fifteen years old when I first helped a slave to escape; and that was nearly forty years ago, long before thee was born.'

He disappeared, to return very shortly with a sheet of paper which he gave to Jack Fairfield to read before he folded it and handed it over to Susanna. The young man read it and nodded amused assent.

'I have nothing to teach you, suh!'

'I wish I could teach thee, Jack, from my own experience, that theft and violence do not pay, even in the best of causes. I love thee, Jack Fairfield; thee has a kind heart and a brave one. I dread to see thee come to a hard end!'

The young man sobered. 'Thank you, suh. Our ways are different and neither of us is likely to change, but I return your love with all my heart.'

Levi Coffin sighed and turned away. He said to Susanna:

'Thee should make haste. The stable is three blocks this side of my store, a little way up the alley.'

Susanna was one of those fortunate people who can remember without effort a road over which they have once traveled. She hurried along, looking up alleyways, and before long saw the sign which advertised in faded letters the ability of the Rammelsberg stable to furnish horses and fine carriages for every occasion.

The hot little waiting-room was a peaceful place. Cobwebs loaded with chaff hung undisturbed in the corners, and the straw littering the floor was never troubled by a broom. Susanna would never have thought any place under the name of Rammelsberg could be so untidy. Beside a glowing fat little stove slumbered a comfortable fat little man, a yellow cat stretched out asleep across his lap.

Susanna hesitated, uncertain how to proceed. She ventured to tap the little man's shoulder; when that had no effect, she patted him more smartly.

The little man straightened up and blinked.

'*Ja, ja*,' he said agreeably. 'It vas that buggy you vanted?'

'I don't know about a buggy — yet,' answered Susanna cautiously. 'I want to see Anton Rammelsberg.'

'I am Rammelsberg, I am Rammelsberg.'

'Then this note is for thee.'

Anton Rammelsberg took the folded paper and turned it over sleepily.

'It does not say so,' he yawned.

'Levi Coffin said so,' Susanna told him impatiently. 'He said to make haste.'

The livery-stable keeper cocked an eye at her with some apprehension.

'Vell, vell,' he muttered, and roused himself to read the note, whispering the words to himself as he went.

'"Dear Friend," — Ach, why cannot every one write the German script I learn when a boy? This American writing, it is hard for me. Young voman, can you read this to me?'

Susanna took the letter quickly. 'It says:

'"I wish to aid some unfortunate colored friends with the use of two good closed coaches for their funeral procession. John Hatfield will furnish the drivers. Kindly have the horses harnessed within half an hour. I will pay the bill. Will thee also give this young woman the use of a buggy at once, with directions how to find John Hatfield at his home, and drive him up to my house where we can make final arrangements about the procession?"

'And he signs it, "Thy friend, Levi Coffin."'

The little fat man shook his head and got slowly to his feet.

'Levi Coffin and mine vife they make me a great deal of trouble. Alvays so much feeling for the black ones! Two coaches! It is an extravagance. But he vill pay the bill, unless the vife hears about it and says No. That is a comfort.'

He dropped the paper into the stove and moved out into the stable.

'You vill have to take this buggy that is already hitched up for the party I vas expecting. And I should know who you are before you take it out. *Ja?*'

Susanna was growing more and more impatient. All her young life she had been brought up to hate slavery, and had been told tales of the Underground rescues. Now that she had opportunity to take part in one of these adventures, it was very trying to be held back by this slow little German, and the explanation she must give him.

'I'm thy niece, Susanna,' she replied, her sober mouth twitching as she looked down at little Anton.

He surveyed her in blank amazement.

'I did not know I had a Qvaker niece yet. *Ja,* vell, I remember now; Frederika vas telling me last night that I had a new niece.'

His face relaxed.

'I am villing. Frederika tells me that you are a goot girl to help, and I am glad she has you. I do not have time for the vork around the house,' he explained pathetically, with a fond glance back at the warm stove and well-worn chair before he devoted himself to giving the girl full directions for reaching the home of the colored preacher. Susanna, who was an experienced driver, was soon rattling away in the buggy.

In all the time that Susanna had to study Aunt Katy Coffin, she was never able to see how she managed to accomplish so much in a short time and with no fuss. The more there was going on around her, the more easily she seemed to work; it only formed a cover for anything unusual she might wish to accomplish unobserved. Susanna thought that this might make some explanation for her keeping boarders, as well as welcoming a constant stream of guests. Under cover of the bustle necessary to care for these, an extra negro more or less, or an unexplained white person on a difficult errand, escaped attention by those outside the household and was not even noticed by the guests themselves.

Now, when Susanna had returned as quickly as

possible with the dignified John Hatfield, she found no especial stir in the Coffin kitchen. Jack Fairfield, clean and dry and extraordinarily handsome in an old suit of clothes that had been found for him, lounged against the wall and regretted amiably that he was of no particular use. Catherine Coffin let him talk on as she tied up a bundle of shoes and woolen stockings inside a roll of blankets. She dispatched the colored man upstairs to her husband, and gave Susanna a motherly little pat on the shoulder.

'Thee sit down here, dear, and have a bite of breakfast. I am afraid Frederika Rammelsberg will have to get along without thee for a little longer.'

Eating her late breakfast, Susanna realized presently that Jack Fairfield was watching her and that he seemed amused.

'For a young lady who is not a relative of the family, it is certainly remarkable how much Miss Susanna looks like a Coffin,' he remarked with great politeness. 'I should have supposed that chin, for instance, was a family mark of identification.'

'Thee likes to tease, doesn't thee, John?' said Catherine Coffin mildly. 'I wish thee would take this jug of hot coffee from under the stove and set it out in the buggy, with a robe to cover it and keep it hot. Then thee can carry out the blanket bundle.

I do not have the bread and meat ready yet, but it will be wrapped soon.'

Susanna was relieved to have him set at these errands. She felt certain she was not going to like this young man; he was not a comfortable person to have around. It was not his affair if her chin were square.

Levi Coffin and John Hatfield were down in the kitchen now, talking earnestly.

'Mr. Coffin, it's like you say, suh: I can't be two places at once even if I am needed at both. If'en you could send some one on ahead with the shoes and provisions, I'd better stay here to lead the procession; I'm a minister and it would be more natural-like.'

Levi Coffin agreed with him.

'We still have our young friend,' he said. 'Susanna is not known as being connected with our enterprise, and so she is as safe as any one we can trust. She does not know the place, but we can give her fairly plain directions.'

He rested his hands on the table and looked down gravely at the girl.

'My child, we are giving thee a heavy responsibility, but I believe thee can do what is needed for these poor people. While John Hatfield finds a few more buggies and the drivers for them, thee will take this one and drive across Mill Creek to the place where the fugitives are hiding. Jack Fairfield can describe it to thee as well as to any one else.'

Susanna stood up at once, but the young man cried:

'I protest, suh! This may be dangerous business. It is certainly no place for a young lady!'

'John, a Quaker girl learns to share all human responsibilities. I would send my own daughter, if she were not known as a member of my family.'

'But, suh, these nigroes are armed!'

'Did thee permit that, Jack?'

'I gave them the guns myself. Far better for them, I told them, to shoot their way through or even to die, rather than be captured and taken back into slavery. You know yourself the punishments they receive.'

'John — my dear John — I do know. But I know, too, that they who take the sword shall perish by the sword. I wish thee could understand that.' Levi Coffin's face was sad. 'Thee sees how much more difficult thee has made it now for those who want to help them.

'Susanna, thee will have to take great care not to alarm the group. Thee seems now in more danger from them than from officers of the law. Try to let them know thee is approaching without attracting attention from any one else.

'Give them the hot coffee and food and distribute the clothing as far as it will go. Tell them that we are sending carriages and buggies arranged to look as much like a funeral procession as possible. That is the only plan we could make to take care of so many at the same time.

'They will go on up the Mill Creek road north past the colored burying-ground, and only a little way farther is a settlement of colored people who can be trusted to take them in and keep them safely until we can send them on up the Underground. John Hatfield will take charge as soon as he comes and then thee can drive home.'

Jack Fairfield gave Susanna painstaking directions how to reach the particular ravine they had chosen as a hiding-place, and told her the names of the leaders of the party.

'Give them my name,' he said. 'I reckon they will trust that as much as anything. I ought to go myself instead of sending you.'

With an anxious scowl on his young face, he tucked the big buffalo robe around Susanna and her load.

The girl drove off, to all appearance entirely calm. The road, edging steadily nearer the river, was easy to follow. One part of her mind repeated the directions that had been given her — 'Third ravine to the right, around a big clump of spice-wood bushes.' Another part was asking suddenly, 'Is this really me — Susanna Coffin?'

It was almost easier to believe that she had become another girl altogether than to imagine her old self, hardly twenty-four hours in Cincinnati, wearing a dress of fine cloth and a stylish bonnet, driving a clean and painted buggy along a road she had never seen, on the unlawful business of helping some twenty-eight slaves to escape from their masters.

The hot coffee jug, jolting against her foot as they went down the hill, brought her out of her day-dream and convinced her that all she was seeing was real. Passers-by looked with curiosity at the big blanket bundle with which she shared the seat, and Susanna had a chilly fear that she might be attracting too much attention. The sight of one or two idling policemen alarmed her more. Under the law it was a matter of duty for them to return fugitive slaves; and there was usually a substantial reward to any one who would return a fleeing black to his owners.

What was it Folger Coffin had said? The Fugitive Slave Law, passed by the Congress of the United States a year or two before, demanded a fine of a hundred dollars from any one found guilty of sheltering, feeding, or clothing an escaping slave, and half of that went to the man who gave the information. Often the slave's master would add a reward to that. It was very tempting to a poor officer with a large family.

Susanna knew that Folger Coffin himself had entertained sneaking thoughts of spying on the

Underground Railway line that ran nearest his cabin; but although he wanted easy money badly he was afraid of the wrath of his neighbors, and contented himself with hoping that his Cousin Levi would some day get his come-uppance under the law. It was discouraging, said Folger, for a law-abiding citizen like himself to remain in poverty, while Levi Coffin, who freely admitted that he had helped thousands of slaves to escape, continued to live in comfortable circumstances.

Well, Susanna had seldom cared for Folger Coffin's opinions. She stiffened her sturdy young back and reflected that she had not yet done anything to deserve a suspicious look from an officer of the law. What came later would be a different matter. In the mean time, she reminded herself, she had wanted adventure, and here it was.

Once across Mill Creek she forgot herself altogether in the anxiety of finding the fugitives. Fairfield's directions had been clear enough, and she could see many foot-marks in the muddy sides of the ravine around the big clump of spicewood, but no one was left there now.

She backed the horse out from the cleared space beside the road where she had tied him and walked on beside him to the next ravine, where a telltale path showed foot-marks again, with regularly a pitiful stain of blood. While she hesitated here the faint, muffled wail of a child struck her ear, and with that for direction she picked up her skirts and went on down the ravine.

Most unexpectedly a man's voice demanded, shakily, 'Who — who dat?'

Taken by surprise, Susanna heard herself stammering,

'Jack Fairfield!'

From a gully above her, heaped with dead leaves, a black man in garments as dingy as the leaves slipped and slid down toward her, gingerly holding a revolver.

'Is you come to help us, Miss?'

'I will if thee will put that gun down,' answered Susanna with spirit. 'I'm afraid of it. I've had a hard enough time finding you and I don't want to be shot now. Is thee Jim?'

The man grinned apologetically and handed the weapon awkwardly to another who had appeared farther down the path at the sound of voices.

'I's afraid of it myself, Missy, and dat's truth; but I's afraid not to have it. We're 'fraid of everything this morning. Dog came sniffin' round the place where Mas' Fairfield told us stay. Des a coon dog he was, but first thing you know somebody hollered "Bloodhound" and somebody else shot that dog; and here we were all runnin' ober here and 'fraid to go back again.'

'Jack Fairfield sent some things for you,' said Susanna. 'Come up the path as far as thee dares and I'll carry them over.'

Her new dress suffered from the mud as she lugged the heavy jug down the path, but the delight on the man's face as his cold hands felt its warmth was quite enough to repay her. By the time that she had brought down the food and the big blanket bundle, balanced over her shoulder, Jim had gained sufficient confidence in her to take her on down to the spot where the women and children perched on the hillside, big-eyed, their faces gray with cold.

Only the mother of the crying baby seemed to take no interest in food after the child had refused to chew a crust. She held it up with its face against her neck to stifle its wailing.

'I heard it crying,' Susanna said to the mother. 'That was how I came to find you.'

'They kept telling me somebody would hear it,' the mother answered wearily. 'Seemed like I couldn't keep her still. Mammy's baby!' she soothed it, holding more closely the unhappy little thing.

'Take this here blanket, Jane,' one of the other women said. 'We don' suffer from cold the way a baby does; though the Lord knows I wish we could have a fire!'

'Do take it,' Susanna urged. 'I'll bring down the buffalo robe for some one else. It was too hard a trip for a baby.'

She was thinking how wearing the night would have been even for a child as old as Tristram.

'It *was* too hard, Miss,' agreed the second woman. 'But they was going to sell Jane away from her baby. She couldn't stand that; she'd do 'most anything first.'

With hot tears in her eyes Susanna brought down Levi Coffin's heavy buffalo robe and had the satisfaction of wrapping it snugly around two thinly dressed women. Then she went back up to the road to keep a lookout for John Hatfield and his procession.

She decided that she would attract less attention from the few passers-by if she untied the horse from his well-gnawed sapling and led him and the buggy over to the roadside, and this she did, with the uncomfortable knowledge that the bushes stirred at the edge of the ravine where some one watched her. These slaves, she realized, were afraid to trust her yet; even now, after she had fed them and explained the plans for their escape, they were ready to prevent her by force from trying to get away from them and betray them.

Knowing this guard and the shaky pistol he probably carried, she was doubly uncomfortable when a kind-hearted farmer stopped to ask, 'Anything wrong with the rig?'

Susanna, who knew how to hitch up a horse as well as any farmer, answered that she thought the check rein was a little high, and the man clambered out of his wagon, adjusted the strap for her with blunt, weather-cracked fingers, and helped her into the buggy before he sent his own team lumbering on. As soon as he was safely down the road, Susanna climbed out again, listening for the little rustle of dead leaves at the ravine edge that would tell that she was still watched.

At last from the distance she saw approaching at proper funeral slowness the carriages she had been expecting. The road was clear. She ventured down the ravine path to find, as she had suspected, that Jim and his pistol were guarding it.

'Can't take any chances, Missy,' he apologized. 'You say they is come? Let me see.'

Fearful and hesitating, the party were persuaded up from the ravine to meet the carriages without delay. John Hatfield drove the first vehicle of the procession, a shining closed coach that was the pride of the Rammelsberg stable. He brought his horses to a stop close beside Susanna's buggy and got down hastily, showing himself in full ministerial black and white. The sight of a man of their own color reassured the stragglers more than anything else could have done.

'Everybody in!' he said, smiling, and opening the door of the coach.

From between the empty seats he took a little black-covered box.

'This here is our coffin. Two of you hold it on your knees so we'll have an excuse to show for our funeral.'

'You go first, Jane,' urged Jim. 'Nice closed carriage! You and the baby git a fine rest and warm up!' But the woman pulled back sharply.

'Don't expect me to get in with that little child's coffin,' she breathed, clutching her baby.

'Well, I don't blame you, Sister,' said John Hatfield benevolently, 'but that little black box cain't hurt you none. My wife fixed it up just before we left and it's full of warm clothes and cookies. Remember we must hurry!'

He half lifted her in. With a catch in her throat, Susanna saw Jane shrinking back into her corner, away from the pretended coffin which two of the women balanced cheerfully on their knees. The baby, tightly wrapped in the old blanket, had at last become quiet.

The procession was soon on its way, at a pace exasperatingly slow to any one who feared for its safety. Susanna did not watch it long. She cramped the buggy skillfully, turned the horse around, and set off for the city at a good pace. She was cold without the buffalo robe; she was tired, too, and she wanted very much to see Tristram.

CHAPTER IV

Jack Fairfield Tells a Story of the Old Days

THE spring came on so swiftly warm that Mrs. Rammelsberg felt herself ready to move out to the summer kitchen in early May. This was a low unplastered shed added to the rear of the already long-drawn-out house, where a third cook-stove, still older than the other two, remained cold from late autumn until spring.

Mrs. Rammelsberg, directing Susanna's stove-polishing while she herself scoured vigorously the white pine kitchen table, cast longing eyes at the wide, blossoming apple tree outside the open window.

'Often I say to myself,' she confided, '"Vy do I spoil this clean kitchen? Vy do I not set my stove under the apple tree and cook there?"' Some day perhaps ve vill do it, you and I.'

Susanna remembered past weeks of cleaning rooms that were already speckless, and was not surprised at this proposal. She was beginning to understand that never would Mrs. Rammelsberg consider her house in good order until it was entirely unused.

'I don't think the draft in the oven would be so good,' she answered cheerfully. 'The cakes might

burn on the bottom and stay raw on top. Coming
up from Car'linya we used to cook over camp-fires,
and the wind was a nuisance.'

'*Ja, ja,*' agreed Mrs. Rammelsberg quickly,
'that is so.' Her affection for good food was almost
as strong as her passion for perfect cleanliness. 'And
the tree might not bear so full vith the heat. Those
apples they are fine for cooking.'

'I like to work out of doors,' Susanna said, half
sorry that she had diverted her employer's mind;
the perfume of the apple blossoms was very sweet.
'I always like to stir apple-butter in the big iron
kettle over an outdoors fire. I've done that in the
fall ever since I was old enough to manage the long
stirring paddle.'

'You like to vork, *hein?*' said Mrs. Rammelsberg,
affectionately. 'Indoors or out, you are a goot girl
to vork. That Hans, I do not know if he vill be so
industrious as his sister. Men are like that. Hans
should go into business; then it vill not matter.
Vat is he doing now?'

'He's watching the cow,' Susanna assured her.
'Five minutes ago I saw him drive her away from
the bed of Easter flowers.'

'Five minutes ago? P-ff! Vat is that?' Mrs.
Rammelsberg had as little belief in Tristram's usefulness about the household as she had in her own
husband's.

Susanna reflected that it might be best to see if

she could find her brother some work away from the Rammelsbergs through the summer. He was growing fast; perhaps Levi Coffin knew of some place where he could be used as an errand boy. She determined to ask him.

She and Tristram both were well-fed and lodged; they were faring much better than they had since that dreadful time of illness in North Carolina; and Susanna was paid two whole dollars a week, which would be quite enough to buy their summer clothes.

The girl had quickly learned to keep herself and their loft bedroom so scrupulously clean and in order that Mrs. Rammelsberg was quite contented; but the scouring of Tristram the German woman felt that she herself must attend to. With her own hands, as she reminded him often, she scrubbed behind his ears every night; nor could Susanna be trusted to see if the boy's bare feet were clean enough to put between Mrs. Rammelsberg's good sheets at night. For this attention Tristram was not in the least grateful; he resented heartily being treated as if he were a baby.

'Show me you are a man, then!' retorted Mrs. Rammelsberg. 'Ven you can vork all day vithout every minute I must call "Hans! Hans! Vere is that Hans now?" then you are old enough to vear your ears dirty if you vish. Though not your feet; never that,' she added hastily, as if afraid Tristram might steal a march on her.

Susanna was leading a double life these days. Most of her time was passed placidly with Mrs. Rammelsberg. 'Hired girl!' she reminded herself, when she wondered, as she continued to do, why Cousin Levi had wished her to drop her own name; but she did not really mind being Mrs. Rammelsberg's hired girl. She was quite big and strong enough to do the work required of her; indeed, she had often worked much harder in the months she had lived with Folger Coffin's family. And she liked to learn from the German housewife, who knew so many ways to cook and crochet and knit; whose preserves and cakes were invariably successful, and whose chickens and cow were always plump and thrifty.

The other part of her life interested her much more, but it never seemed quite real; when its incidents were past, she was never certain that they had really happened or that anything of the kind would ever occur again outside her dreams.

At Mrs. Rammelsberg's order she would go down to the Coffin house with a basket of eggs or butter or young pie-plant; and what would come next she never knew.

She might be asked to sit by the kitchen table for a little while and then sent on a walk with a woman dressed in the height of fashion, whose heavy veil hid a black or a brown face. Twice she had done this, losing her companion when, at some distance from the house, a buggy pulled up by the curb and took her in, flashing swiftly away up the street bound for the nearest Underground Railway station outside the city.

Once she had escorted a spectacled colored mammy to Mrs. Rammelsberg's to stay overnight until she could be started on the road to Canada. In the safety of her home, to Frederika Rammelsberg's great disgust, the fugitive had with much chuckling disclosed himself to be an old colored man who boasted of the success of his disguise until he nodded asleep.

'Dey lookin' for me all right. Dis ain't d' firs' time I try to get away; dey cotched me befo'. But dey ain't lookin' for an ol' woman. Nossuh! I come up on d' boat. I tell 'em I's trabbelin' Nawth to my Mist'ess, an' dey say, "Poor Mammy, ol' an' nea' blind! Let huh sleep on d' floo' of d' ladies' cabin!" Ho! ho!' He laughed till he had to take off his precious spectacles and wipe the tears away.

Mrs. Rammelsberg, like all her fellow Germans who were lately settling that corner of the city, was heartily opposed to slavery. She did not often go down to Catherine Coffin's weekly sewing circle for clothing fugitive slaves, but every week she set aside an afternoon for such sewing at home; and to these clothes she often added small sums of money for the Coffins to use; but she could not bring herself to want the poor creatures, ragged and dirty, in her own home.

'It is not their fault,' she told Susanna the next morning, boiling the sheets the old man had used in a froth of soapsuds, 'but they are not clean. No! They are not! I hope Mr. Coffin vill send me no more.'

One of Susanna's excursions became the occasional meeting of the early morning river packet from Louisville to Cincinnati. Gradually and cautiously she was told the whole story of this stage of the Underground passage to the North. A mysterious and unnamed friend of Levi Coffin lived in the Kentucky town down the river, it seemed. It was known that he was ready to help an escaping slave, though the difficulties in a slave State were great.

He had, however, worked out a simple plan that was used many times over. When the time seemed most convenient, he would engage a stateroom on the boat that plied the Ohio River from Louisville up to Cincinnati, and would take the key for it under his own name or one of his invention.

A little while before the boat left Louisville, while there was a great bustle of passengers and baggage on the wharf, along the gangway and in the boat itself, the slave who was attempting escape would be sent on board with his bundles as if he were bringing them to his master. Once on board some one would give him a signal as to the room engaged for him. where he found the key on the inside of the door and promptly locked himself in. With fare and berth both paid for, not even an officer of the boat had any right to disturb him, and he might listen securely to the splash of the paddle-wheels until the boat docked in the morning by free soil.

Susanna understood that the Louisville man used to accompany these fugitives and bring them up from the wharf to the Coffin house, but that now he was so much under suspicion that he no longer made the trip.

Instead, after the stateroom had been engaged, he sent an innocent-sounding telegram to Levi Coffin. Sometimes it said, 'Pay forty-three dollars to Dr. Peck on my account,' or 'Go to Box seventy-two at the post-office and take charge of letters found there.' Rooms in the ladies' cabin had even numbers; those in the men's cabin odd numbers. If the telegram gave an odd number, some man, though rarely Levi Coffin himself, met the river packet; if the number were even, he might send Susanna down to the wharf, giving her word the day before so that she could go down very early and not possibly miss the arrival of the boat. When the steamer tied up at the landing, it was Susanna's part in the little play to walk aboard quietly but with her head well up, as if she belonged there, to knock four times slowly on the stateroom door of the number telegraphed, wait until the door was opened, and then walk away followed by the colored woman, apparently her slave.

In the general confusion of unloading the boat,
she had never yet been questioned, though she was
beginning to wonder if the purser did not recognize
her. From the boat she went up the street, followed
by her humble shadow to some place of refuge.
Sometimes she was told to go to a tenement in the
negro quarter of the city, where the woman was
expected; sometimes to the house of Levi Coffin or
to one of his white friends. There seemed to be an
increasing number of these latter who were willing
to take in fugitives, in spite of the strict laws pro-
hibiting such help. Once the slave was safe inside
the door, Susanna went home to change her good
dress, eat breakfast, and attack a day's work.

She remembered now that she must tell Mrs.
Rammelsberg that she could not help with breakfast in the morning.

'When I took the clabber-cheese down this morning, they gave me a number to meet to-morrow,'
she said, straightening up to view the shining stove
with sober pleasure.

'The *Schmierkäse?* Vas Mrs. Coffin pleased? I
thought it vas maybe a lee-eetle tough. You should
have taken it off the stove a minute sooner; then it
vould have been so nice and smooth.'

She looked over at the tall girl with a worried
wrinkle between her eyes.

'I think Mr. Coffin sends you to the boat too
often. I must tell him so. It is not that I cannot

spare you, though you have learned to make the breakfast coffee as vell as I myself do it; and Hans, he is alvays a better boy ven you are here. But I am afraid they vill get to know you on the ship. Six times you have been down. Mr. Coffin should find some one else. You may get into much trouble.'

'It's hardly daylight when the packet gets in,' Susanna reminded her, 'what with the fog in the river bottoms. And the officers are all so sleepy that they are not much interested in the passengers.'

'Sleepy, *ja*; but cross. Should they find out vat you are doing they vould not be kind even to a beautiful young lady. And the sun rises earlier every morning, but the boat comes in at the same time.'

'I've thought myself,' Susanna admitted, 'that it might be better to send some colored man on board who would be taken for a porter.'

Frederika Rammelsberg nodded vigorously.

'You have right, my Susanna; you have right. You are brave. Do not be reckless!'

Susanna had time enough to think over this advice, as well as plenty of other matters, while she waited next morning for the boat to steam in. This time waiting was more tiresome than usual, because of the rumor she had overheard that the boat had stopped to pick up more freight and would be late.

She wished that Levi Coffin did not insist on her being near the landing so long before the boat was expected to dock. There was no waiting-room open at that hour, and she was afraid of becoming too well-known a figure if she stayed down on the wharves, where she enjoyed watching the boats and the big river. Usually she walked with great dignity around the near-by streets, wishing her unfamiliar veil did not tickle her nose so much and listening for the screech of the steamboat whistle.

This morning, as she turned aimlessly down toward the open space of the river front, she saw a little farther on a tall figure, surprisingly familiar. Susanna's eyes opened wide. She forgot she was a dignified young lady, as she picked up her wide skirts and ran to catch up with the young man sauntering slowly ahead of her.

'Jack Fairfield!' she cried, finger-tips on his coat-sleeve, and then flushed hotly at his downward look of surprise. Perhaps he had forgotten her altogether.

'I hadn't seen thee since — since ——' she faltered.

The old charming smile flashed out to reassure her as the young man lifted his hat and made her a bow.

'No, not since then. It might not be safe to go on with our reminiscences here in the open street, Miss Susanna. I have your name properly, I hope. Or

has our friend, the Railway President, given you
still another?'

'I'm still Susanna,' the girl murmured, hurt and
embarrassed.

Jack Fairfield regretted his mischief.

'Forgive my teasing. I can't ever seem to out-
grow it, though I must be ten years older than you,
and you so well-behaved! But you see you are a
Quakeress, with a Quaker father and mother and no
end of Quaker grandparents. Now I am only a
Virginian; that makes a lot of difference.

'What are you doing here so early?'

'I'm meeting a boat,' Susanna answered, uncertain how much more she might tell, but there
seemed to be no need of further explanation.

'You will certainly be tired before the packet
comes in. Let us go down to the wharves, Miss Susanna, and watch the boats while we dream of lost
romance and present adventure!'

He offered his arm and Susanna shyly laid her
hand on it. He was dressed, like any fine gentleman,
in the best of cloth and ruffled linen, and Susanna
might have been afraid of him if she had not remembered him, dirty, wet, and ragged, in the Coffin
kitchen.

On the top of a new barrel, whose staves smelt of
fresh pine, he spread a great silk handkerchief cere-
moniously and helped Susanna to perch herself
upon it, and for a time the two watched in silence
the wakening river traffic.

Presently he shook his broad shoulders as if throwing off an unwelcome mood.

'It's too late,' he said. 'It's too late.'

Susanna looked up startled through her veil.

'I was only thinking,' he explained, 'that if I had lived thirty or forty years earlier I might not have been the bad boy I am now! I shouldn't have gone around stealing other people's human property. There would have been adventure enough for me, Miss Susanna, almost anywhere in this new country; just on the river alone there were the most amazing happenings. I could have had even more excitement than I wanted, without bringing a frown to the brow of a law-abiding citizen. Even Levi Coffin might have approved of me!'

He regarded her quizzically, evidently wondering what she would be provoked to say.

'There were some of the river men he wouldn't approve of,' she answered with unexpected spirit. 'When we came up from North Car'linya two years ago they used to tell stories around the fire at night about Simon Girty and Mike Fink. I think the children were more afraid of them than of the Devil himself!'

Jack Fairfield laughed. 'I didn't suppose you knew the river tales. I will admit that Mike and Simon were not the best of citizens or even of river men. But there were others who had adventures, too, and all within the law. Did you ever hear

about the first steamboat to come down this river?
No? Let me tell you.'

His face was keen with interest.

'One of the men who was shipped on that boat as
deckhand told me the story not so long ago when
we were traveling up to Canada together. We had
to stay hidden in a barn for three days while the
slavers hunted us and he kept me amused by telling
me the story of his life.

'He was a white-haired old negro. This tale goes
back forty years and more to a time when Cincinnati was nothing but a little backwoods town. The
old man lived then in Virginia, not far from Pittsburgh, at the headquarters of the Ohio River; once
before this, he told me, he had floated down the
Ohio and the Mississippi to New Orleans on a flat-
boat, and there were hundreds of miles of river-
bank at a stretch without a single settlement.

'Old Joe had a hazy idea that this was the first
steamboat to ply on American waters, but I've
made inquiry and found he was mistaken. Two of
them, at least, had already been successful on the
Hudson River, and Mr. Fulton was anxious to try
his new invention elsewhere.

'But I reckon he and his backers were just a little
wary about risking their lives among the bears and
alligators that were supposed to fill the Middle
West. At any rate, they found an adventurous
Dutchman in New York State, by the name of

Roosevelt, and he agreed to go down the Ohio and the Mississip' to see if a steamboat could be expected to navigate those waters.

'When he returned after some months, saying the thing could be done, they told him to go ahead and build the boat at Pittsburgh and launch it there. They sent him a metal-worker and ship's carpenter who had helped build Fulton's first boat, the Clermont, and the two worried along together, until, in October of 1811, the new boat was ready to take to the water. They christened her the New Orleans.

'Young Roosevelt had directions from his company back East to proceed with the boat to Natchez. It was intended to ply back and forth between that town and New Orleans. There was not enough trade farther north. He took no freight or passengers down-river, only his young wife and their bran-new baby; then there was the engineer and the pilot and a few hands, including old Joe, who told me the story.

'I gathered that for the first few days Joe was afraid for his life aboard this noisy new contraption; but pretty soon, he said, he got used to the noise of the engine, and then it was great fun to see how they alarmed the settlers along the river. Most of them had never heard of a steamboat before, and they took it to be anything from a floating sawmill to a falling comet. There was a comet plain in the skies that autumn, he said.

'One of the hair-raising things about the boat was its steam-whistle. Old Joe said that when they rounded up to the Louisville bank on a still moon-light night and saluted the town with a blast from their whistle, every inhabitant of the town jumped from his bed to see what had broken loose.

'Young Roosevelt had naturally feared trouble with his engine, but Joe did not remember that it took more than the ordinary amount of tinkering. All their hindrances came from natural causes. When they reached Louisville they found the river so low that they could not proceed over the rapids. For a few weeks they waited, making short trips back and forth between Louisville and Cincinnati, until the people along the way no longer jumped out of their skins at the shriek of the whistle. Then the fall rains came and the river rose; they scraped over the rapids and were off.

'Of course all the river boats burn wood now, but there were no wood yards along the river then, and Roosevelt didn't want to send the hands ashore to cut wood whenever the supply ran low. When he had made his previous trip down-river, he had noticed some coal banks and he had got permission to work them as the boat came to them, and use the coal as engine fuel.

'The first coal bank was on the Indiana side of the river, and since he had bought it from the Indiana Government he was right provoked to find, when he tied up there, that somebody had already been working his coal mine. But it might have been worse. Whoever it was had been scared off after the coal had been brought down and dumped on the shore. The hands of the New Orleans had only to load it on, without lifting a pick-axe.

'While they were taking the coal aboard, some squatters came down from their cabins, so scared that they did not even pay any special attention to the steamboat. They said that there were strange noises in the woods and on the river-bank, and that the river-banks had been shaking. Joe felt right sorry for them. They were all poor whites, thin and sick-looking, and Joe decided they must have been having chills and fever so hard they thought the earth was shaking with them.

'The New Orleans got her full load of coal and went on, with the crew laughing at those poor ignorant Hoosiers; but the next day they did not feel so superior.

'It was queer weather, very warm for November; they could see the sun, but it sent down little light, as if it were misted over. And every now and then a large part of the river-bank would tear away from its hold with a rush and a splash and be lost in the yellow water.

'Then Joe remembered that he had heard a preacher say the Lord never meant man to use machines to tear around at high speed from one place to another; and he was afraid God was angry with the boat. He wished he could escape, but the land seemed now even more dangerous than the boat, supposing he could have reached it.'

'What was the matter?' Susanna asked innocently.

Fairfield might have begun the story with the idea of whiling away time for his companion, but by this time he was, himself, entirely absorbed in its happenings.

'What — why, an earthquake!' he answered, with a glance of surprise, and returned at once to his narrative, which the girl did not again interrupt.

'The next day was still worse. The pilot gave up then and said he was lost. As many times as he had floated down the river, he did not know it now. Where he had always found deep channel, there were drowned trees with their roots upward. The word crept round the boat, and some of the men who had grown sick with watching the trees waving on the bank, though there was not a breath of wind, went to Roosevelt and asked him to return to known country and solid ground.

'Roosevelt was worried about his wife and baby, but he thought that there was a fair chance of finding clear channel in front of them as the river widened, and he knew that behind them there was the confusion of the earthquake. And they steamed on.

'That night they were much put to it to know
where to tie up till daylight. Usually they had
brought to under the shore, but the high banks were
still caving in, covering flatboats and rafts aban-
doned by their owners. The pilot thought it might
be better to stop by a large low island that he remembered hereabouts in mid-channel, but when
they looked for the island they could not find it. It
had disappeared into the river.

'At last they stumbled onto a small island and
tied up to the foot of it, taking their chance of its
lasting through the night. No one slept much. The
water roared and gurgled, and every so often a
splash told of land and trees swallowed up. They
were all sorry for Mrs. Roosevelt, shut up in her
cabin with the little baby. At the first dawn they
cast off. The water was rough, but the motion was
not so sickening as the trembling of the land.

'None of them knew where they were by that
time, either by the look of the shores or of the river
itself, but it turned out that they were near the
mouth of the Ohio, and about noon they came to a
little town called New Madrid, on the west bank of
the Mississippi.

'There had been a settlement at that spot ever
since the days of the Spanish, and the inhabitants
must have felt fairly secure, even though the country about was still full of Indians and wild animals.
Then, overnight, their houses had begun to fall

over their heads and the earth opened round them in great cracks, spouting waves of sand. The New Orleans found the whole site of the town slowly sinking and nearly deserted. The people, who were camping on higher ground, begged to be taken on board, but Mr. Roosevelt would not take passengers. If the land was unsafe, so was the river, and his responsibilities were already heavy enough.

'He ordered steam up and the little boat struck out again, dodging uprooted trees, watching for contrary currents, and prepared for almost any happening.

'Joe told me the whole story twice over, and then he added an extra touch, though he said he feared I would consider him a hopeless liar.

'Not long before they came to New Madrid, he said, suddenly the river current changed and the little New Orleans was hurried back up the river so fast that his old cap was nearly blown off his head. This reversal lasted only a moment, and then the current gradually returned to its ordinary direction and speed; but presently they came to a wide rapid across the Mississippi, which looked exactly as if the water were pouring down into some wide crack in the river-bed. He was so frightened that he did not know how they ran this rapid.

'All the way down to Natchez he dreaded being seized again by this fearful force; but after they left the New Madrid neighborhood, they saw little more of the earthquake except for the floating trees in the swollen current, and they reached Natchez in safety.

'When he went back to Virginia he walked. No boat for him! He walked every step of the way!'

CHAPTER V

The Purser is Surprised

JACK FAIRFIELD had been talking with his eyes directed absently far down the river, as if he could see in the distance the New Orleans chugging along on her maiden voyage. Now he turned gayly back to Susanna.

'Now don't you see how it is with me?' he said. 'I was born out of my time. If I could have been Mr. Roosevelt on that trip, I should have had enough to think about to keep me out of mischief then and for a long time afterward!

'But there have never been any more first-class earthquakes; and steamboats are common things. If I get the adventure I crave, I have to lead my present life, which our friend, the President of the Railway, assures me is wicked and will bring me to a bad end.

'Wouldn't you have liked to be on the New Orleans that trip, Miss Susanna?'

'I don't know,' Susanna answered honestly. 'It is an interesting story; but how did the Roosevelts get home to New York? And how were the woman and the baby after that awful trip? It must have been hard to get anything to eat along the way, and she would need fresh food.'

Fairfield's quizzical amusement softened to a smile.

'I never thought about that part of it, I must confess. I believe that Joe did say that the Roosevelt family took a boat from New Orleans up the Atlantic Coast to New York. He was afraid of getting taken along, and he had had enough of navigation for the rest of his life. But he never told me about the health of Mrs. Roosevelt and the baby, and I didn't inquire.'

'The baby thee helped bring across the river that night died,' Susanna told him in a low voice, her eyes full of tears.

'What? I'm sorry to know that. I hadn't heard since that day from the immortal twenty-eight. Were the rest of them all right?'

'Yes. A letter came from Canada, so we know about them. But the baby — thee knows it was cold and sick and it cried. So the mother wrapped it up tight in a blanket. Maybe it was wrapped too tightly, but it was quiet and she didn't disturb it for fear it would cry again, and direct too much attention to them all. And when they got to their first stop, it had died.' Susanna was glad of the veil that hid her trembling lip.

'And so the funeral procession was a real one after all,' Jack commented. 'Our friend, the President of the Railway, is favored that way. I'm sure he never tells a lie. He says so. But not all of his

words and his schemes are quite what they might
seem to an officer of the law, though they never
catch him in deception.

'Well, it's all in a good cause, and I admire him.
I do, indeed. But I wish he would not scold me so
for my sins!'

Susanna made no answer, and he drummed
thoughtfully on his knee.

'Well, he was right about one thing. I ought not
to have tried to bring so many over on that trip.
We might all have been drowned. But every one
begged to come, and the baby's mother most of all.
I could see her point. The baby had no chance at
all if she were sold down the river. It wasn't a
strong little thing.

'Besides ——' he straightened himself, and
though his tone was still low it was boastful, 'besides, it was too good a chance of paying Kentucky
back. That evened nearly a whole month of my
score.'

'What does thee mean?'

He looked disappointed. 'I might have known
that our friend was too discreet to tell the story
even to a person he trusts as he does you, Miss Susanna. It was like this: Most of this winter I spent
in a Kentucky jail for nigro-stealing. It was a bad,
cold winter, too. If I hadn't found two or three
men that were Free Masons like myself, I'd have
been there yet, but they helped me to break jail

before my case came to trial. I got away and over into Ohio, and there I had lung-fever for a while in peace and quiet.

'The Railway President was good enough to come see me there; and he told me that the best thing for my health would be to go to store-keeping in Canada for a good long while, but I couldn't agree with him. I was too sick and too mad. I told him that I was going back to Kentucky, and for every day they had held me in jail, I was going to help a slave escape. And I've made a good beginning!'

Susanna was alarmed. The scattering crowd of steamboat hangers-on, waiting for the delayed packet, were eyeing his gestures with too much curiosity. She slipped down from her barrel and folded Fairfield's handkerchief carefully before she handed it back to him.

'I thank thee very much for the kerchief — and the story,' she said, with a primness that quite checked any further confidences. 'When Brother has a cough like thine,' she added earnestly, 'I always put goose grease and red flannel around his neck. And I make him keep his feet dry!'

'This cough is nothing,' the young man said indifferently, 'and if it were, Aunt Katy has given me enough cough remedies to cure an army. Goodbye, Miss Susanna. There is your boat. I hope I haven't bored you too much.'

He bowed and slipped away through the swarm
of yelling porters and hackmen, without a backward look. The packet's gangway was lowered
with more than the usual haste, and Susanna had
little time to wonder if she had been rude.

She followed her usual routine. The crowd leaving the packet was impatient with the delay and
hungry for breakfast. So was Susanna; she could
understand and make allowances for the pushing
and shoving of the passengers. What she did not
like was the scowl of the purser. This was the boat
she had met most often, and she made up her mind
that this must be the last time, for she felt certain
that the man recognized her.

Fortunately he was busy, and he said nothing to
her. She hurried back to the ladies' cabin and
knocked slowly four times on the door whose number had been given her, saw it open, and an indistinct veiled head nod at her; and then she walked
very slowly back.

Some one blocked her way as she came to the
last door. It was the suspicious purser, his under
jaw thrust out determinedly, an ugly look on the
face he thrust close to Susanna's. Even in his
swagger uniform he looked dirty and ill-kept; Susanna could see that he was very tired, and his
breath told her that he had been drinking.

The girl glanced quickly over his shoulder to see
if she could find any one who would help her. She

did not want to appeal to any other officer of the
boat, for fear of trouble for the woman who was
following her; but in any case there was no officer in
sight. The last of the passengers were hurrying off
the gangway, and she could see only porters loaded
with baggage and stewards intent on putting the
boat in order and finding a little rest for themselves
before it set off again. She would have to depend
on her own efforts. The purser scowled and held his
place.

'Please let me by,' said Susanna. 'I am ready to
leave the boat.'

'I'll bet you are,' sneered the man. He braced
himself against the doorway. 'I've seen you before.
I remember folks, I do. What's your game? I know
you never came up from Louisville as a passenger.'

'I came on board to meet a friend who is a
stranger,' answered Susanna, remembering that the
veil she had seen through the crack in the door had
been thick and the dress below it respectable.
'Please let us pass.'

'Unhunh,' said the man. 'Yeah. Let's have a
look at your friend.'

Susanna stiffened. She knew now that her first
fear was correct; that the purser suspected her of
helping a fugitive slave.

She had one more resort; tied in the corner of
her handkerchief was a silver piece that she had
brought in the expectation of buying Tristram his

SHE FOLLOWED HER USUAL ROUTINE

long-promised stick of peppermint candy to replace
the stick he had lost on his first day in Cincinnati.
Susanna unknotted the money quickly and offered
it to the purser's shaking hand.

He only laughed.

'Keep it, lady, keep it. I don't want small
change. I want real money. Tell your friend back
there to put up her veil or I'll do it for her.'

He roused himself to push past the girl, but he
reckoned without the solid muscle Susanna had
developed in hard and heavy work. Susanna set
herself squarely in his path, determined to stay
there, and quite certain of being more than a match
for his half-drunken fatigue. She dreaded the row
that would follow; the picture flashed across her
mind of herself thrown in jail for 'nigger-stealing'
and of forlorn Tristram weeping under her prison
window; but she felt that at all costs she must protect the woman waiting back in the shadow of the
passageway, who was depending on her for freedom
and safety.

'Git out of my way if you don't want to be hurt,'
snarled the purser, and then wondered what was
happening to him.

A long arm had reached in through the doorway,
swung him violently around by one shoulder, and
dragged him out into the empty deck beyond.

A voice familiar to Susanna demanded, 'Suh,
were you addressing my wife?'

Susanna gasped.

The purser was not so easily brought to sense.

'I don't know whether she's your wife or not,' he answered, glaring up into Jack Fairfield's angry face. 'But I know this: If she's bringing slaves through from Kentucky, she's liable to arrest, whoever she is, and I git the reward.'

'Suh,' said Jack Fairfield, 'you are speaking to a Virginian!'

The man was a little taken aback; he stopped struggling in Fairfield's grasp to look him over and comprehend that he was dressed like a gentleman.

Susanna stepped back very cautiously; she thought that she might be able to get the veiled woman past while the purser hesitated, and indeed they were nearly at the door before the purser was aware of them. Then, to Susanna's horror, he whirled around, breaking from Fairfield's hands, and roughly jerked back her companion's bonnet, pulling the veil with it.

'Now then ——' he began, triumphantly, but he stopped in the full course of his speech, as if some one had laid a hand across his open mouth.

It was very well for the others that he was too astonished to notice them, for he could not have helped seeing that the face under the veil was as surprising to them as it was to him.

The woman, whose arm Susanna held, lifted indignant gray eyes to the purser; her clear complex-

ion was flushed, and the tumbled hair under the
displaced bonnet, though dark, was as soft and
straight as Susanna's.

The woman promptly took charge of the situation.

'Sir,' she addressed the staggered purser, 'have
you any excuse for such treatment of a lady who is
a passenger on your boat? I should have remonstrated before, but I could see that you were in-
toxicated and I hoped to avoid a scene with a
drunken man. I regret now that I did not; but I
shall report you to the company and ask for your
dismissal. Come, Sally!' she called to a colored
girl, apparently her maid, whom Susanna had not
seen before; and followed by the maid who carried
her handsome bags she sailed down the gangway
with fine insulted dignity.

'My Lord!' moaned the purser. 'Was I that
drunk?'

At this Jack Fairfield woke from his own amazement.

'Now,' said he, 'I'll show you what we do in the
South with poor white trash like yourself when they
insult women.' But the purser had taken alarm at
the first word and was off into the dark recesses of
the ship as fast as he could scuttle on his shaky
legs.

Jack's fist slowly relaxed and the old mischie-
vous smile came back to his lips as he looked down
into Susanna's bewildered face.

'Good riddance!' he said. 'Now let us find the mysterious lady. My guess is that she may need some directions. And, in case any one was listening to our little scene, will you take my arm?'

He lifted Susanna's fingers to the crook of his elbow and escorted her down the wharf with great ceremony.

'That was great fun,' he said. 'I feel quite cheered up. What would you have done — er — Susanna?'

'I would have stayed right where I was,' the girl assured him. 'He wasn't strong enough to push me out of the way, and I don't think he would have dared to hurt me.'

'H-mm! I'm not so certain about that. I think I shall have to tell our friend that you aren't to meet any more boats.'

The woman, her bonnet and veil again in order, was standing not far away, bargaining leisurely with a cabman.

'I think the fare is a little high,' she answered to Jack's polite inquiry as to whether they could be of service to her. 'Perhaps, sir, if you and your wife are going in my general direction we could share the cab and its expenses.'

'Nothing would please Susanna more,' Jack answered sweetly. 'You will excuse me, I know. I must attend to some matters of business downtown this morning.'

He saw that they were seated in the cab and that the cabman was supplied with Levi Coffin's address, and he stood bareheaded as the cab rattled away.

'A handsome man, your husband,' the lady observed graciously to Susanna.

'He isn't my husband,' Susanna made haste to answer, blushing red. 'I don't know what made him say that ——'

The lady smiled.

'It doesn't seem so surprising to me, when I look at you. And, of course, it gave him a better right to protect you from that awful purser. I nearly got you into serious trouble. I am sorry.'

Susanna tried to stammer out the question that had troubled her ever since she first saw her companion's face.

'Thee isn't —— Is thee a —— I mean, I suppose thee is just bringing this girl through?'

'The cabman can't hear,' answered the lady calmly. 'Yes, I am a slave, if that is what you want to ask; just as much of a slave as Sally is.'

'I didn't know there ever were white slaves,' Susanna murmured, embarrassed.

The lady lifted her eyebrows thoughtfully.

'I don't think it is harder for me to be a slave, with my white skin, than it is for Sally in her pretty brown one. In many ways my life has been easier. Sally had to work in the fields and has been

whipped more times than she can remember. I did
fine sewing, and I never was struck in my life.

'The cabman is stopping. Is this the right place?
It was very clever of the young man to help me out.
I had no idea where I was supposed to go next.'

With much grace and assurance, attended by
Susanna, followed by the maid and the cabman with
his arms full of baggage, she swept up the walk to
Levi Coffin's front door.

CHAPTER VI

Some Underground Ways

IN her short acquaintance with Levi Coffin, Susanna had learned that her relative was the most careful and cautious of men. He showed none of Jack Fairfield's love of adventure for its own sake; the dark-skinned, frightened fugitives who came to him for help were sent on to Canada under methods as safe and business-like as he could make them; and if it seemed necessary in an emergency to take some reckless step, he did so without any flourish, so that it usually seemed the most natural thing to have done.

After Susanna's experience with the purser on the Louisville packet, he did not send her to meet any more boats; that was not a necessary risk. It was even a good while before she was again sent through the streets with a runaway dressed in a disguise invented by Catherine Coffin. Susanna hoed the young cabbages in the Rammelsberg garden, made new shirts for Tristram, carried down fresh vegetables and butter to the Coffin house and carried the empty basket back up the hill.

But, to her intense surprise, she found that Rose, the lady of the boat adventure, was the guest of honor at a kind of continual reception at the Coffin house these days.

Levi Coffin gave whimsical invitations to his friends to come in and see a curiosity that he had lately received from the South. Not only did he invite those Cincinnati citizens that he knew to believe in the abolition of slavery, but he also invited acquaintances who had told him plainly that they had little sympathy with his views on the evils of slavery.

They came politely, though stiffly. After one glance at Rose's beautiful face, they sat on the edge of their chairs, staring like small boys, and wondering if some trick were being played on them. This woman a slave! Impossible!

Levi Coffin looked on with a twinkle in his eye as Rose endeavored courteously to put them at their ease.

'It's a shame, Mr. Coffin! It's a shame!' they would say hotly as they left his parlor. 'A white woman like that a slave! You — you can rely on us not to give any information about her to the authorities.'

'I feel certain I can depend on thee,' Levi Coffin would answer, shaking the hand of his visitor as if they had just concluded a bargain; and the man would go away, wondering just how much he had promised in his excitement and indignation.

Some of them felt it better to keep out of Friend Coffin's path for a while after that, fearing that he might actually call on them for some real help to his unpopular cause; but others returned, bringing friends whom they asked permission to introduce to Rose, and secretly slipped a little money into Levi Coffin's hand as they went away.

This exhibition of Rose as an instance of what slavery might be was perhaps not so rash as it appeared to Susanna; the Underground Railway found several new friends who were taken with Rose's beauty and accomplishments; but Susanna was really alarmed. She was almost as uneasy when Rose was sent over to Lawyer Joliffe for a few days' visit, during which he brought in several of his lawyer friends and a judge or two. The question of fugitive slaves was coming more and more into the courts, and sympathy there counted for a great deal.

It was a relief to the girl when Rose herself decided that she ought to be going farther north, bade them all an appreciative farewell, and departed like any other lady, on the train. Sally, her brown companion who had played the part of her maid, had been sent on by the usual Underground Railway plan, driven from one country town to another, always under the cover of darkness and in the protection of trusted men; and it had not been considered safe for her to stop this side of the Canadian border. But as for Rose, they heard presently that she had established herself in Detroit as a fashionable dressmaker, and would be glad to have them visit her!

Catherine Coffin wrote down the address. 'Some day we might go there,' she said. 'Levi plans to visit Canada again some day.'

'Where did Rose get the money for traveling?' Susanna ventured to ask. Susanna had so little money of her own that the question was a real puzzle to her. 'Did she tell thee?'

'Yes, indeed! They always seem glad to talk to some one they can trust, poor things! When she was just a girl she had been hired out by her owner, an elderly man, to a pleasant family that were fond of her and good to her. They educated her and had her taught fine sewing; and she learned good manners just by living with them and seeing how they treated the servants and each other.

'Then one day they had word that the old man who owned her had died and that his son, who had inherited his property, wanted her back. He was moving to the State of Mississippi and would take her along.

'Well, thee knows the reputation of plantations in the Far South. The work in the fields is hard and the overseers are said to be cruel. Rose could not feel that she ought to go.

'Besides her wages, that this family had paid to her real master, they had often given her sums of money. She had more than enough saved for the fare to Cincinnati. She thought that the dear woman she lived with knew what was in her mind.

for she asked no questions about her packing, and when Rose left she kissed her and gave her a little purse of money. Thee knows Rose was very self-possessed, but she could hardly speak of that good woman without tears.'

Altogether, Rose's stay in Cincinnati was without question a successful occasion. For some time afterward it was understood that a faint, quizzical smile on Levi Coffin's sober mouth meant that he was thinking about that visit, perhaps remembering some uneasy caller and his astonishment that a slave could be a handsome woman that 'you couldn't tell from white! No, sir, nobody could!'

It was while he was in this unusually expansive mood that Susanna undertook to speak to him about Tristram, who grew daily more resentful of Mrs. Rammelsberg's 'Hans! Hans! Vere *is* that Hans?' and the endless excellent instruction that she gave him.

Not only did Frederika Rammelsberg believe that a healthy girl ought to do outdoors work, but she also believed that boys might be called on for housework.

Tristram did not mind helping Susanna; he loved Susanna so dearly that he did not even mind sprouting dusty old potatoes with her. But he felt an abused household drudge when Mrs. Rammelsberg tied an apron tightly round his neck and set him to stemming strawberries with a steady flow of

directions not to drop any berries on the floor, not
to eat any, not to overlook those that the robins had
pecked, and 'Hurry, Hans! *Ach,* vy are boys so
slow?' He ate his luscious strawberry pie later with
an ungrateful heart.

On the morning when Susanna had last met the
boat, she had returned to the house, tired from her
unusual excitement, to find that Tristram had disappeared altogether. After some hunting she found
him dug into the hay of the tidy little barn, quite in
fugitive slave style. He sobbed that he was waiting
for nightfall to come when he meant to take old
Whitey and run away. Tied up in a rag he had
four cold soda biscuits already well mashed to
crumbs and a pocket knife that Anton Rammelsberg had given him on one of his rare daytime ap-
pearances at home.

Tristram had had an unusually trying time that
morning in Susanna's absence; so hard, indeed,
that he felt he could no longer bear it. Mrs. Rammelsberg had decided that he ought to learn to
make a feather bed.

'She said, supposing my wife was sick, would I
want to live in a house with the beds not made? I
don't like feather beds, and I'm never going to *have*
a wife,' said Tristram.

Susanna knew that Mrs. Rammelsberg's fine
goose-feather-filled ticks were the pride of her
heart. It never occurred to her that they were hot

in warm weather. Susanna slipped hers off her cot at night and slept on the cool, hard straw mattress, but Mrs. Rammelsberg never guessed this; if she had found it out, she would have thought less of Susanna, who could not appreciate a fine bed. No wonder that she considered the making-up of the bed important.

On the other hand, there were difficulties in arranging a feather bed so as to present a beautiful, puffy, even surface. With Tristram's short arms it was almost impossible.

A feather tick was not stuffed full like a pillow; it held just enough feathers so that the body sank down, down into the bed with a cushiony billow on either side. Every morning the tick was turned over and the feathers vigorously punched and patted and smoothed into place. The inexperienced bed-maker was sure to find that all the feathery contents of the tick had gone to the head, leaving the foot limp and thin, or that some corner had flattened out like a pricked balloon. The problem was to coax the feathers to lie within the tick in an even, fluffy layer, and over that to float sheets and blankets and coverlid without disturbing the feathers as they were arranged; and, last, all the covers must be tucked in firmly on sides and at the foot, still without making a dent in the perfect surface.

Tristram had not been able to do all this, even if he had wanted to. He did try, but the more he tried

the less successful had he been, and the oftener had
Mrs. Rammelsberg pointed out his mistakes; until
he had finally flung a pillow into the very middle of
the bed and run away.

Susanna pointed out to him, before they climbed
down from the haymow, that he was an ungrateful
child, as she felt she should, and she saw to it that
he promised to try to please Mrs. Rammelsberg;
but she did not blame him very much.

She thought the matter over well and consulted
Tristram a little later, when, one summer evening,
they were gathering early pale-red cherries in the
thrifty young orchard.

'Wouldn't thee like to have a real position, perhaps be an office-boy, or learn some trade? I don't
know whether thee could earn any money at first,
but thee is growing so fast that thee might soon be
paid.'

She had wondered if the country-bred boy would
like this idea, but Tristram had forgotten his first
dislike of the town, and was now only anxious to
see more of its excitements and become a real city-
dweller.

In his eagerness he almost lost his hold on the
smooth cherry limb.

"'Sanna! Could I? Could I get away from that
ol' German woman? 'Sanna, could I be Tristram
again?'

'I don't know,' answered Susanna, hastily steadying him by his stout shirt-collar. 'I'll have to find out what can be done. Brother! Don't thee spill those cherries!'

Next morning, bright and early, when she carried down a great pail of the cherries to the Coffin kitchen, she plucked up courage to address Levi Coffin as he was about to start for the store.

'I want to speak to thee about my little brother,' she said, clasping her work-stained, capable hands behind her and looking straight into his eyes, very like her own for steadiness and keenness.

'I hope thee knows that I am grateful to thee for placing us with Mrs. Rammelsberg. She has been good to us. We never did have so much to eat, or such good clothes to wear, even back at home; and I have learned a lot from her. But Brother isn't happy there.

'I think, perhaps,' Susanna confided, 'that boys oughtn't to be with women-folks all the time. They don't understand each other. Mrs. Rammelsberg thinks Tristram is lazy, and he thinks she nags him, and it seems to me that each of them makes the other worse.

'I asked Brother if he wouldn't be glad to learn a trade or have a job as office-boy. And he would. He would be very glad. Could thee help him, if it isn't presuming too much on thy kindness?'

'Learn a trade? How old is the child?'

'He is just going on ten. But he is growing fast.'

'He must go to school again,' said Levi Coffin decisively. 'I couldn't consent to bind him out to a trade that would take his whole time. But I might find a place for him as an errand-boy with us this summer, till the fall term of school opens. Can thee recommend him?'

Susanna nodded earnestly. 'Brother is a good boy. He just needs to work under a man. They don't scold so much.'

'Not all women scold,' said Levi Coffin kindly, 'Catherine doesn't, and I'm sure thee doesn't. But send the boy down to my store in the morning and I will try him out myself running errands.'

'I do thank thee,' Susanna told him.

'Thee is welcome. The boy may make a good business man. It runs in the family. Has thee met Cousin Charles Coffin, back in Indiana? He was put in his father's bank when he was only twelve years old, and he is a successful banker now, though I dare say he is not more than thirty.

'Maybe thee has heard of the new boarding-school he is interested in up there. It will be a good thing for our Quaker children. Perhaps Charles wishes he had gone to school longer himself, though he has made good use of his spare time and is a well-read man.'

'I heard of it,' Susanna assented slowly. 'I did use to wish that Brother could go there some day. But of course he has to earn his living.'

'There are other things even more important than earning a living,' her relative answered. 'Well, send the boy down in the morning. I shall do what I can for him, though I can't see far ahead these days.'

He took up his broad-brimmed hat again, but Susanna held her ground a little longer.

'Brother will want to know about his name — what thee wants him called. Mrs. Rammelsberg calls him Hans, but he doesn't like it.'

'Hans is a very good name,' said Levi Coffin disappointingly, set his old hat firmly on his head and went off about his business, leaving Susanna's spirits sobered.

Apparently Tristram must now be told that he was to continue as little Hans Rammelsberg, and Susanna understood very well his rebellion against the name. She herself answered obediently when addressed as Susanna Rammelsberg, but she called herself plain Susanna. Circumstances had not yet forced her to give a name that was not her own, but she did not expect to escape it forever. In her mind she saw herself and Tristram going through life as Rammelsbergs and resting at last with the long name carved on their tombstones. It gave her a queer homesick feeling.

Kind Catherine Coffin must have seen and understood her wistful look.

'Susanna,' she said gently, 'will thee carry this

hot water and these cloths upstairs for me? I have
my hands full.'

Susanna followed her with the clean cloths and
steaming pail up two flights of stairs to the attic.
She had never penetrated the Coffin house so far
before. Catherine Coffin knocked on a door and
opened it, leaving Susanna outside.

'It is no one thee needs to fear, Charley,' Susanna
heard her say. 'This is a friend of ours and of Jack
Fairfield's. She is helping me this morning. Thee
may come in now, Susanna.'

On the little cot inside a black man lay. The arm
outside the covers was bandaged and one knee was
propped up on a pillow. Susanna helped to wash
his face and hands, to straighten the covers of his
cot, and place some food on a little stand where he
could eat it, though awkwardly, with his uninjured
hand.

'I'm afraid thee finds this room a little warm,'
Catherine Coffin apologized as they were leaving.
'But it does seem to be the safest place for thee.'

'Beats lyin' in the swamps,' he answered, with a
broad flash of white teeth. 'I feels like I was in the
top story of heaben!'

'Has thee time to seed a few cherries for pies?'
the older woman asked when they were down in the
kitchen again.

'That man thee saw just now,' she went on
quietly, 'was brought here by John Fairfield a little

while before Rose came. There were seven or eight others, all strong, intelligent men, but ragged and hungry. This man was wounded, and some of the others had small hurts, but not so serious that they could not be given medical attention and food and clothes and sent on to a safer place.

'They said John had told them that he would take them out of slavery or die in the attempt, if only they would stick with him; and they agreed that they would all die together rather than be captured. John gave each of them a revolver and ammunition. Thee understands that I do not approve of that; I am only telling thee how this man came here.

'They said that they were fired on several times by the patrollers looking for escaping slaves. They usually fired back, and they always escaped. One moonlight night, when they were starting on from the field where they had hidden all day, they came onto a bridge where armed men lay concealed at either end. Once the slaves were fairly on the bridge they were fired on from both ends at once; but they kept their heads and charged forward, firing as they went, and the patrollers scattered.

'When John Fairfield first began bringing fugitives up here, my husband didn't believe half the stories John told him about his adventures. It is easy to see that he enjoys telling a good story. I could see that Levi thought Jack might be exagger-

ating his tale of the fighting, but Jack showed him
their hurts and the bullet holes in their clothing.
The poor man upstairs had a fever in his wounds
from lack of proper care.'

'Was — was — Jack Fairfield hurt?' Susanna
asked, seeding cherries industriously.

'A bullet had grazed his arm, but the wound was
healing nicely.'

'When — when I saw him at the boat he looked
all right,' said Susanna in a small voice.

'I have no doubt of it. He had left a little money
here with us, and after he had rested he bought new
clothes, and looked very fine in them.'

'Has thee heard from him since then?' Susanna
could not help asking. She did not like to think of
Jack Fairfield wounded; perhaps he would get a
fever in that scratch, from his encounter with the
purser.

'No, dear child. But I think he would let us
know if he were very ill or needed help badly. He is
proud and independent, but I think he loves us.
When he had the lung-fever this winter, he sent
word to us and was very glad when Levi went to
visit him, though he would take none of Levi's advice. Nor will he take my cough medicine, though
he should, with that cough still hanging on, and so
much exposure to wet and cold.'

She finished the elaborate pattern she was cut-
ting in the top piecrust, lifted it and laid it neatly
over the cherries.

'Now I was telling thee about the man upstairs. Thee may have wondered why we let Rose be seen while she was here; but people felt sympathy for her when they would have felt none for a slave whose skin was black; and on the same account it would have been fairly easy to send her off in case of danger.

'But Charley, upstairs, is not so fortunate. He is quite valuable as a work hand, too, and we hear that there is a considerable reward offered for him by his master. The marshal has not asked for him here, but the longer he stays, the more danger there is of his being found. But, on the other hand, he might be crippled for life if we sent him off before his wounds are healed. So thee sees we must be very careful about any information that gets about. Not even the boarders have found out that he is upstairs.'

She slid another pie into the oven and turned to regard Susanna earnestly over the top of her spectacles. Her cheeks were flushed by the oven heat, but her white cap and apron were in perfect order and there was not even a dust of flour on her gray dress.

'Thee sees, doesn't thee, Susanna, that different methods must be used for different cases? And if thee feels impatient with some of them, thee must remember that they seem the best at the time.

'We are watched, and any one by the name of

Coffin would be watched, too. I do not believe thee knows what bitter feeling is often shown against us. Levi believes that it is always safer when possible to make use of what he calls a cat's-paw, or of some one who is nct known to have any connection with us.

'Now thee came here where no one knew thee as a Coffin, so thee could go about without suspicion falling on thee; and thee has been able to help the poor slaves as thee could not have done under thy own name. Such excellent help as thee has given is hard to find in any case. We appreciate it, and I may say that I do not think thee will be sorry in the end that thee gave up thy own name for a while.

'We will say no more about it now, but will thee think it over?'

'I will,' promised Susanna, and surprised herself as much as Catherine Coffin by stooping to place a warm kiss on the soft cheek.

Taking the long walk home she made up her mind to patience. Greater events were going on about her than she, with her youth and lack of experience, could realize. She would do what she was told, so that she would not hinder their march.

But how was she to explain to Tristram?

CHAPTER VII

Tristram's First Job and First Fight

WHEN Susanna announced that Tristram was to be tried out as errand-boy at the Coffin store, Mrs. Rammelsberg was almost as delighted as the boy himself. From that moment his difficulties with her grew so much less that he hardly remembered he had any at all. He was even allowed to wash his own neck before he started to work in the morning, only being compelled to report to the housewife for inspection and invariable orders to scrub again under the left ear.

In the evening he returned, tired with excitement, but pleased with himself, and glad to be at home again. Mrs. Rammelsberg beamed at him and gave him an extra helping of chicken and dumplings when he told them that he had been promised the tremendous wages of fifty cents a week if he continued to work as well as he had done that day.

'That Hans, I have alvays said he is a fine boy!' she told Susanna. 'Has he blacked his shoes for to-morrow? I vill mineself iron his clean shirt out to-night. It is no trouble.'

By reason of his work downtown, Tristram had become a man for his women-folks to wait on,

rather than a child always at the call of his elders,
and Tristram thoroughly liked the change.

He poured out to Susanna endless accounts of
what he had seen and done in the city. She heard
all that he knew about the errands he ran and the
people he met.

'Thee must be careful,' Susanna cautioned him,
'not to talk to everybody thee sees about all these
things. Thee might tell some secret about business
or the affairs of the Railway.'

'I'll keep my mouth tight shut,' Tristram promised, and Susanna, knowing his shyness, felt it
would probably be much easier for him to be silent
than to chatter.

As the summer weeks went on, he reported regularly with his fifty cents wages, which were far too
precious and hard-earned to be spent at once. The
money was put away, and it was understood that it
was to be used for school books.

Tristram seemed to have only two grievances
now. One was that he still disliked to be called
Hans. An innocent person, calling to the tow-
headed boy, 'Here, Hans!' was likely to be astonished by a cold, indignant glare turned on him by
the boy before he trotted off to accomplish the requested errand. Susanna was troubled, too, that he
did not get along well with the boys who most fre-
quented the neighborhood of the store.

The boy in the green trousers, who had made

Tristram's first day in Cincinnati miserable by chasing him down the street, was employed not far from the Coffin store; and Tristram could never see him without remembering his lost stick of candy.

And Tristram saw him often, not only as he went up and down the street on errands, but between-times when the boy had nothing better to do than to stop by the door to tease the newcomer. He was older than Tristram, and, though he was not more than two or three inches taller, he was much heavier. Tristram was afraid of his superior size, and still more of his malicious tongue. The one comfort that he had was that the boy did not remember having ever seen Tristram before. Tristram's hair was now cut by a real barber, instead of Susanna's shears, and his clothes, though plain, were no longer of Quaker cut, but in the style that any other city boy of the times might have worn.

The boy seemed almost friendly when, one dull morning, he stuck his round face inside the door to look for Tristram.

'Hey, you!' said he, when he had spied the younger boy standing as bravely as possible behind a counter. 'Come on out! Show you a game!'

'Can't,' Tristram answered briefly.

'Can't nothing. Where's your old man?'

Tristram had no intention of letting the boy know that both Levi Coffin and the clerk were absent for a few minutes, leaving directions for Tristram to ask any customer that might come in to take a chair and wait. Instead he turned his back and made a show of rearranging a pile of bolts of calico.

'Aw, come on,' the boy coaxed. 'Here's a game I learned.' He fished a pair of dice out of his pocket and rattled them in his palm.

'Don't want to,' said Tristram.

The boy eyed him as if he had some thought of pulling Tristram out to play by main force, but he was too lazy. Instead he bent his fat legs in their long tight trousers and seated himself in the door.

'What's your name?' he demanded.

Tristram bit his lip and was silent.

'What's the matter with you?' the fat boy asked, exasperated. 'Why can't you talk, hey? My name's Billy. Ain't yours Hans?'

'That's nobody's business,' choked Tristram.

Billy was delighted. He did not know what the trouble was, but he could see that he had made the stubborn small boy angry.

'Why ain't it? Ain't that what they call you? Sure it is. I heard them.'

He began to experiment with a tuneless little song, apparently addressed to the other side of the street.

'Hans, Hans,
Made of cans!

TRISTRAM SAW HIM OFTEN

'Hansy, Hansy,
Was a pansy!

'Hans, Hans,
Thought he was a ma–an!'

There is no telling how many more verses he
could have invented if he had not been unexpectedly interrupted by a shower of missiles. Tristram was not an experienced fighter; he used no
science; he merely gathered up anything that was
loose and flung it at the fat boy's astonished head.
By the time Billy could pull himself to his feet,
there was a very floury cloth bag draped over his
head which partly protected him from the contents
of the dust-pan which Tristram had sent after it.
A well-wrapped ham, which the clerk had laid
under the counter until the customer who had
bought it came for it, followed the dust-pan; but it
was too heavy for Tristram to manage easily and
did little damage to Billy.

The broom was still left handy. Tristram charged
out from behind the counter with it, handle first,
straight at his tormentor's plump stomach, but
Billy had by this time recovered himself enough to
guard and dodge.

'Thee get out of here!' Tristram shouted furiously. 'Don't thee ever come back here again!'

'Why, you ain't German!' gasped the fat boy.

'Neither is thee!' retorted Tristram, driving the

broom handle home to Billy's middle and sending him tumbling out on the sidewalk.

'You're Quaker!' the boy accused Tristram, picking himself up and brushing off flour, lint, and street dust.

'Get out!' shouted Tristram, lunging again with the broom; and the other thought it wiser to leave, muttering surprising threats as he moved off.

Tristram found himself left alone, waving the broom, hot and tear-stained; and suddenly he felt rather silly. He swept up the floor of the scene of battle, returned the uninjured ham to its hiding-place, and folded up the empty flour sack very carefully. He also washed his hands and face, but hastily, for fear some one would return and catch him at the suspicious task.

His conscience was beginning to hurt. Suppose the boy should tell on him and he should lose his position and the fifty cents a week. Suppose he should have to go back to Mrs. Rammelsberg's and learn to make beds. He knew very well that no good Quaker fought; he 'lived in that spirit which takes away occasion for war.' Tristram had not lived in that spirit and he felt himself to blame. At the same time he knew all too well that he would be just as angry when he was called Hans again. With these thoughts flurrying in his brain, it was no wonder he washed only the center of his face and had to be sent back to finish by the clerk when he returned; but the clerk only wondered why boys' faces were always dirty.

To one thing Tristram made up his mind: He would continue under the name of Hans, because Susanna had wanted it, and he would endure whatever teasing came on that score; but he would not be teased for being a Quaker. So far as he could he would stop being one in public.

His plan was simple. All his life he had been brought up in a Quaker family and a Quaker community where plain clothes were worn and the 'plain language' spoken. These people used the 'thee 'and ' thy' that their ancestors, English farmer-people, had used before them for hundreds of years. They refused to give the complimentary plural 'you' to one person, in the days when the use of 'you' still meant a real compliment; nor would they use titles. The King himself was plain Friend Charles to them. Further, they replaced what they called the 'heathen' names of the months and the week-days with simple numbers. January, the month of Janus, became First Month; Thursday, the day of old Thor, became Fifth Day.

The difference was little, but it was enough to make their speech noticeable. To some of the people who dealt with the Quakers, their dress and speech were the outward signs of a pleasant simplicity and honesty; to others the difference seemed unnecessary and ridiculous, and with these poor Tristram now agreed.

His clothes contented him, but he would have to learn to speak in everyday language, which he had heard old Friends call the 'world's language'; and to that he devoted himself. Susanna was mystified at his continual muttering to himself.

'Sunday, Monday, Tuesday, Wednesday, Thursday, Friday, Saturday!' Tristram recited under his breath. 'You, you, you, you ——'

It was not long before he had learned his new language and could keep the new and the old separate. To Susanna and in the store he still said 'thee'; but outside his 'you's' rattled off glibly.

Of his encounter with Billy he never told Susanna, nor did he explain to her his exercises in language; but since he must tell her something as they went about their evening chores, he began to try to remember more of the serious conversation that went on above his head, and he was rewarded by Susanna's intense interest.

'They're worrying about the Fugitive Slave Law,' he reported one evening.

'They've been worrying about it for more than a year now,' Susanna said.

'Maybe so. But they say some cases will come up pretty soon now. The first in the something-or-other. This district, I guess it was.'

'I wish Mrs. Rammelsberg took a newspaper,' said Susanna. 'But of course she doesn't read English well enough to enjoy it. There might be something in the paper about this. I tell thee, Brother, I'll see if I can go down to the store with thee in the morning and ask Levi Coffin about it. I think he would tell me. And thee can show me what thee does at the store.'

Tristram looked up at her admiringly as they started off next day in the fresh summer morning.

'Thee — thee is pretty, 'Sanna,' he told her. '*I* think so!'

Almost any one would have agreed with him. To her plain crisp dress of lavender-sprigged white Mrs. Rammelsberg had generously added a linen collar which she herself had embroidered, by which Susanna's healthy outdoor coloring was well set off. She worked in the yard and around the garden too much to acquire a fashionable mincing step, or to tolerate tight shoes and skirts that swept the ground; and now she walked along with a freedom that was pleasant to see.

'Thee looks handsome, too, Brother,' she answered gayly.

'Am I, really, 'Sanna?' he asked wistfully.

He was beginning to wonder if there was something odd about him besides his speech. In spite of his efforts to change himself so that he would look and behave exactly like any other Cincinnati boy, he was still teased and tormented. Billy never tackled him alone, but there seemed to be plenty of others who were willing to add their voices to the

fat boy's, or to throw apple cores after Tristram and
then scurry, hooting, down a convenient alley.

Tristram tried to walk through these attentions
without noticing them, though it was hard. He had
a faint understanding of the real state of affairs; it
had become the fashion to tease Tristram, and the
fashion would have to wear itself out or be checked
by some plan more startling than Tristram had
been able to invent. He knew better than to try a
fight again, with the enemy in such numbers; besides, he had no real interest in a planned and prepared fight, such as it would have to be. If Tristram
were ever to be dangerous, it would have to be when
he was driven by sudden and real emotion.

There seemed to be nothing for him but to endure; though he could not help keeping a childish
hope that some day he would be able to show them
all that he had points to be admired.

'Doesn't thee like those boys?' asked Susanna,
noticing that he glanced without speaking at those
they met.

'No!' said Tristram. 'And they don't like me.
I wish I could fix 'em!'

If Susanna had asked questions then, she might
have found out more about the difficulty; instead,
disapproving of the tone of his voice, she said,
'Tut!' and Tristram kept his secrets to himself.

Early as it was, a group of men had already gathered in the back of the Coffin store. They seemed

to be waiting; there was not much talk among them.

Susanna began to lose her confidence at this sight of business afoot; she wondered if she had not been overbold in coming to ask about a matter in which she had not been consulted.

'It's — it's a public matter,' she told herself in as grown-up style as she could, but, when Levi Coffin came up, she only said meekly, 'I don't want to bother thee. Thee seems busy.'

'Not yet,' he answered. 'We have a committee meeting called, but not all the members are here yet. There is a New England family in town on a concert tour, and they have offered, if we will arrange it, to give a concert for the benefit of our treasury. With all the expenses of this trial of Louis, it is getting sadly low. Did thee want something?'

'I wanted to know about the trial,' Susanna blurted. 'Brother said he heard there was to be one, but he didn't know anything more about it. The Rammelsbergs never have a newspaper. I thought it might be important, and that thee might not mind telling me. It's — it's a public matter, isn't it?' she finished bravely.

So far as his quiet face showed, Levi Coffin seemed both pleased and amused.

'Thee is right; the matter is anything but secret; though there are not many people who know the whole story. Thee ought to know it. The trial is really of great importance and we are watching it closely. The decision that the Commissioner makes to-day will affect all the other decisions about fugitive slaves that come later.

'Thee sees, some of us have known Louis before, so we take a personal interest in his case. He ran away from his master in central Kentucky several years ago, and made his way up to Cincinnati. He settled down here in the city, feeling safe on free soil, as he had more reason to do before Congress passed the Fugitive Slave Law in '50. We found him employment, but after that he never needed help; he worked and took care of himself.

'Then he went up-State to Columbus, but there he ran across some one who knew him and sent back word to his master. The master went after him and had the Columbus marshal to arrest Louis — they can't refuse to arrest under this law — and the three of them started back for Kentucky and slavery.

'Louis had friends in Columbus who telegraphed to Lawyer Joliffe, and he called me in, and we arranged a little surprise for Louis's master. Most of the States have laws of their own that conflict directly with this Federal law. Ohio, for instance, has a law providing that any slave who comes into the State with his master's consent is free thereafter; and we knew that Louis had once come up to Ohio with his master to take a drove of horses back to Kentucky.

'We took advantage of this Ohio law to meet the party when they left the train at Cincinnati with a writ arresting the master himself for kidnaping a free man. I can say that he was very much surprised and quite indignant. He had to leave Louis here in the jail for safe-keeping, while he went on home to find witnesses who would say that Louis is his property.

'Now he is back with his witnesses, and a great array of special Kentucky marshals, to see that we anti-slavery men don't become violent.' He smiled at the idea of himself engaged in deeds of violence. 'The case has been on trial for several days and we expect a decision to-day.'

'A favorable decision?'

Levi Coffin shook his head doubtfully.

'Commissioner Carpenter is a conscientious man, but the law is against the fugitive. The statement of the master is practically all that it requires. I have not much hope.'

An active, eager little man had come up to them.

'Mr. Coffin, our committee is slow in meeting. I think I'll just step over to the court-room and see if anything is happening there yet.'

'Use thy own judgment, my friend. Jonathan Cable expected to be here before this time, but he is a busy man and no doubt he cannot help being de-

tained. I should not advise going on without him,
for he may be able to help us find a good place for
the concert if we should decide to give it in a church.
Not all his fellow ministers would dare take in an
anti-slavery concert.'

The little man turned to go; but Levi Coffin de-
tained him.

'Samuel Alley, this young friend is taking a real
interest in the trial. Would thee have the kindness
to let her go over with thee? She may see something
of importance. Susanna, would thee like to go over
to court?'

Susanna nodded, while her heart missed a beat
with excitement.

'Not much to see yet, I reckon, but we'll find
out,' said Samuel Alley amiably. 'I get so worked
up, I have to go over and look in, every once in a
while. That's the French of me, I guess. Mr.
Coffin stays quiet as a mill-pond; and you take it
easy, too, don't you, Miss? Well, I like to see folks
keep their heads, even if I don't.'

CHAPTER VIII

Levi Coffin Wears his Hat to Court

SUSANNA had no idea where the little man was to take her. She was prepared to walk any distance necessary to attend the trial, but Samuel Alley bobbed in at the door of the building just next door down the street.

'You know the new court-house ain't finished yet; takes a long time to put up a great building like that; so they just hold court around where it's convenient. This trial's going on up here in Wilson's building, second floor.'

He cupped a hand under Susanna's elbow and gave her quite unneeded assistance up the stairs. Susanna felt herself very much a grown-up lady.

She stood soon inside the door of a long bare room, whose most conspicuous furnishing was a table, a good deal like a store counter, down the middle. A few cheap wooden chairs were ranged along either side, with one armchair placed precisely in the center, its back to the door. Over at one side stood twelve more of the little chairs, close together in two neat rows, facing the table. Samuel Alley hurried over and brought one of these for Susanna.

'Jury seat,' he explained to her. 'This ain't a jury trial; it's just the say-so of the slave-owner and that's all. But the janitor's sort of half-witted, and he forgets. Every night he fixes the chairs real nice for the jury box, ready for next day. It's got to be a joke with some of us.'

He considered the situation. 'Now you want to see the people come in and you want to see the judge and you want to see Louis. Kind of hard order! I guess we'll set you near the end of the table. I don't know as I'd stay too long, if I was you. There'll be a raft of folks in; *big* crowd! Oh, there's a man I want to see!'

He darted off, leaving Susanna seated well out in the room, like a little island. She pushed back a little and looked about her. The man that Samuel Alley had hailed was a person that she had sometimes seen at the Coffins'; he must be an abolitionist. There was no one else that she recognized in the slowly filling room.

Small groups of men drifted in at the open door, looked around as if they hardly expected to see anything, and soon braced themselves against the wall or planted their feet wide as if for a long stay. The room buzzed with their talk; the Southern inflection trailed past harsh Middle-Western voices, and groups of anxious colored men whispered to each other and tried to keep out of the way.

'Wonder there's not a fight,' drawled a man near Susanna.

'Too many marshals in the room,' another an-

swered. 'They've been keeping pretty strict order
in court session, and you see that they have an eye
around now, even though court hasn't convened.'

'Plenty of difference of opinion in the room,' the
first said, looking with narrowed eyes around him.
'I nearly knocked a man down myself this morning
for telling me a nigger couldn't be property.'

'Oh, give the law a chance,' the other grinned.
'Maybe after this decision we'll know for sure
whether a man's property is his own or not. It can't
come out but one way.'

'Well, it's pretty bad,' the first grumbled, 'when
a man can spend his good money for slaves that skip
out whenever they take the notion. I hope this law
has teeth in it! Why, nigger-stealing is worse than
horse-stealing!'

His friend consulted a large silver watch. 'Here,
it's not nine yet,' he yawned. 'More than an hour
before court is supposed to set, and no telling what
delays after that. Lord, what a crowd!'

Samuel Alley had completely forgotten Susanna,
as well as his committee meeting. He stood, argu-
ing earnestly, where Susanna could watch him
pounding his right fist emphatically into his left
palm, but the sight gave her little comfort; she felt
very much alone in this sea of strange men. It was
with great relief that she heard the rustle of silk
skirts beside her and looked up to see the face of a
woman she had met before.

'It's Mrs. Cable,' said that lady. 'My husband's the Presbyterian minister, you know. I've seen you at Mrs. Coffin's. Jonathan came to his committee meeting late as usual, but there was still another member missing. Mr. Coffin brought me over to see the trial and to keep you company, my dear.'

Susanna rose at once to give Mrs. Cable her chair, but she had turned and was watching the doorway.

'There was a special marshal at the door as we came in. They have brought several men up from Kentucky to act as marshals during this trial and I hear that they have been officious and hard to get along with. This one seemed to recognize Mr. Coffin from the other days of the trial and to want to keep him out.

'Oh, Mr. Coffin, what did that horrid man want? I thought I had better run away and leave you, in case of trouble.'

Levi Coffin answered patiently: 'There was no real trouble. The marshal asked me if I were a witness, and why I was going in.'

'And what did you tell him? He is still frowning.'

'I told him the truth — that my business was my own and not his, and that we live in a free State on this side the river. Will thee excuse me? I see Samuel Alley over there.'

'My! My!' Mrs. Cable breathed in admiration. 'Can't he say and do the most outrageous things in the calmest way? Jonathan is daring enough, but he isn't Mr. Coffin's equal.

'Yes, I'll take the chair, Susanna, thank you. We can change when you get tired.'

She settled her wide silken skirts around the little chair and peered alertly around her, naming over to Susanna people she knew.

'Here comes that marshal now,' she announced suddenly. 'What does the man want? He seems to be after Mr. Coffin again. I'm so afraid of trouble before this trial is over.'

'Take off your hat!' the man commanded. And more loudly, 'Take off your hat, I say!'

'What is the matter?' Mrs. Cable whispered, wonderingly. 'Oh, I see; they must be expecting the judge soon. They're clearing the way from the door. But why such a fuss?'

Susanna was trembling. She understood better than Mrs. Cable what might happen now. All over the room the few hats that had been worn indoors were coming off as a sign of respect to the opening of court. But Susanna had been well taught that to the Quaker, for many years back, his broad-brimmed hat had been a symbol, like his 'plain language.'

He would not doff the hat to those supposed to be in authority over him; no, not to royalty itself. He removed it in respect only when he addressed God in prayer at times of worship. William Penn had worn his hat in audience with King Charles II; Susanna knew very well that Levi Coffin would not take off his hat at the command of a Kentucky marshal.

The Kentuckian had by this time reached the Quaker, where he stood, still talking to Samuel Alley.

'Take off your hat, suh!' he repeated angrily.

Levi Coffin looked at him coolly. 'What is the matter with my hat? I suppose it will not hurt any one?'

That corner of the court-room hushed, and his voice carried distinctly.

The marshal, finding himself under observation, evidently made an effort at self-control. 'Suh,' he said, 'you are in the United States Court. I have authority here. I command you to pull off your hat.'

Levi Coffin replied serenely: 'I shall not pull off my hat to accommodate thee. It is not my habit nor the habit of my people to make obeisance to men.'

The marshal's fist clenched. 'Pull off your hat!' he growled. 'I tell you, you are in the United States Court.'

The older man looked up at him with a little pity.

'I do not see that Court has convened yet, though it seems about to. I may be more familiar with the United States Court than thou art, my friend. I have served on juries in different courts, and in various States, but never yet have I been commanded to pull off my hat; and I am not aware that a Commissioner's Court, trying a fugitive slave case, is a more sacred place than other courts.'

The marshal had reached the limit of his patience under the eyes of the crowd. With one angry sweep of his arm he jerked the offending hat from the Quaker's gray head. 'Take it!' he said, thrusting it at the owner.

'I thought thee wanted it,' said Levi Coffin quietly, turning his back on the man, and leaving him in full possession of a hat which he did not know how to dispose of.

The conversation that went on while he stood turning the hat in his hands was not on a subject that would ease his mind either, since it was a discussion of the possibility of holding another meeting of the committee for the benefit of the slave on trial; but the marshal was a little wary of starting another argument. He looked around the room helplessly and at last laid the hat on a broad window-sill near by and went back to his post at the door.

Mrs. Cable nudged Susanna.

'He looks like a hound that has been successfully defied by a rabbit,' she whispered with great enjoyment. 'He was not expecting that from a Quaker.'

Susanna still watched uneasily. A Cincinnati policeman had come up to Levi Coffin now.

'Mr. Coffin,' he said, with the trace of a smile on

his face, 'wouldn't you better be getting your hat
now? It's lost it might get, with all these strangers
around.'

'Thank thee for thy interest,' said Levi Coffin,
'but I did not put it there, and I shall not go after
it.'

'Well, then,' said the policeman amiably, 'I'll be
after getting it for you, sir. It's a good hat, I dare
say, and the price of a new one would make you
that much poorer.'

He pushed through the interested crowd and
brought over the hat, dusting it carefully and shap-
ing up the crown with a quizzical eye.

'I'm not sure of the Quaker style, sir; but it
seems to have come to no harm. There you are!'

Levi Coffin took back his hat without haste, and
promptly set it square on his head. 'I thank thee!'
he said to the amused policeman, and returned to
his conversation.

Back by the door the marshal seemed to have
plucked up his spirits. He had, by loud questioning,
so frightened a few visitors that they had retreated
back down the stairs. Now his eye swept the room
and rested again on the restored hat.

He wasted no time. 'Pull off that hat!' he roared,
and, seeing that the owner paid no attention, he
squared his shoulders and brushed through the
crowd, now rather startled.

'Pull it off and be quick about it!' he ordered,

when he had reached Levi Coffin. 'I told you this was United States Court!'

'And I told thee,' said the other, 'that I have often been in courts before, both in this country and in the English dominions, and I have never before been commanded to pull off my hat. Friends have been permitted to approach kings and emperors with their hats on; we do not bow to men. I generally take off my hat for my own comfort when I am in a house, but I do not wish to take it off now. It is not uncomfortable, and I do not intend to stay here long.'

The marshal scowled.

'Pack of nonsense!' said he. 'You're one of that bunch of Quakers that's been helping slaves escape. Ain't you? Ain't you?'

'Since thee asks me,' returned Levi Coffin blandly, 'I have sheltered and fed a number of poor creatures who *said* they were fugitive slaves; but thee knows the word of a slave is not good in a court of law, so, of course, I was not bound to believe them.'

At this amazing statement, Samuel Alley suddenly doubled over with a burst of laughter that he vainly attempted to muffle, and around the group who heard ran a disrespectful grin of appreciation. Even the Kentuckian near Susanna whispered to his friend, 'Got him there!'

The marshal was past speech. He clenched his

teeth, jerked the broad-brim off, and started elbowing his way to the window. The crowd fell back, but a threatening murmur arose, 'Better not try that again!' 'That's more than I can stand!' 'And I won't stand it, either!'

The marshal never reached the window; his path was blocked by the big city policeman, one hand out.

'Let the gentleman's hat alone, you, sir! Give it here!'

'Who are you?' muttered the marshal.

'Don't be asking who I am. I'm a city officer, sir, and I have as much authority as you have. Faith, and I use it better, too. You can get back to your place if you have one!'

He turned to the calm-faced Quaker with a bow. 'Now, sir, Mr. Coffin, here is your hat, and I hope you have no more trouble from them as should behave better.'

'And I am obliged to thee again,' answered Levi Coffin. 'Good-bye, Samuel. I shall expect thee this afternoon at two o'clock at the same place.'

He clapped his hat on his head and made his way out of the room, past the red-faced marshal, who pretended to be looking in another direction.

'We-ell,' sighed Mrs. Cable, 'we were so interested in Mr. Coffin that we didn't even notice the judge and the lawyers had come in. They'll be bringing Louis now.

'I always enjoy watching Mr. Coffin in action, though I could wish Jonathan wouldn't imitate him. He had the sympathy of the crowd, didn't he? The marshal seemed like the villain of the piece, and yet he may have thought he was doing his duty.'

Court was formally convened. The judge and the lawyers were seated at the long table with their backs to the door through which they had entered the room. Opposite them sat the colored man, Louis, whose case was on trial, with his master on one side of him and the marshal from Columbus on the other. The crowd moved closer to the table to see and hear, and Mrs. Cable stood up.

'I can't see a thing,' she whispered to Susanna. 'These Kentucky men are so tall and I'm so short. I wish it weren't undignified for the wife of a Presbyterian minister to stand on a chair. Susanna, why don't you climb up there and tell me if anything happens? There seems to be nothing in particular going on yet.'

Susanna was a tall girl, but even she could see very little through the forest of broad shoulders between her and the end of the long table. Standing on a chair in public might be unladylike for a young woman of sixteen, but it would have great advantages for sight-seeing. She lifted her lavender-sprigged skirts and was soon a head above the men around her, who smiled indulgently if they noticed her at all.

The judge was in no hurry to begin the reading of his long-awaited decision; while he consulted his notes and requested information again on certain points, Susanna's eyes wandered over the room. By this time half of those there must be anti-slavery men. Back by the door and out in the hall were a good many Cincinnati Germans; she saw Anton Rammelsberg, looking fairly wide awake, among them. There were a surprising number of colored men along that side of the room, taking comfort from the friendly nearness of the sturdy Germans. Grouped around the chair of the slave, Louis, were a number of white anti-slavery men, bent on giving him such silent sympathy as they could.

All this information Susanna whispered down into Mrs. Cable's upturned bonnet.

'Have they got Louis handcuffed? Can you see that?' the kind-hearted woman asked. 'He was brought to court in irons the first day, and the Commissioner ordered them taken off. I was afraid they might put them on again to-day.'

No, Susanna reported, his hands were free.

She liked the slightly built brown man who sat there waiting. He looked worried, but not frightened, and he listened to the discussion between the judge and the lawyers with evident intelligence.

A little bustle at the door caught Susanna's eye. She started to speak to Mrs. Cable, but thought

better of it and kept very still. Past the marshal at
the door the Reverend Jonathan Cable was making
slow progress, his hat firmly set on his head.

One experience had not been enough for the
marshal. 'Take off your hat!' he demanded.

Jonathan Cable went on.

'Take — off — your — hat!' the marshal said,
his voice rising.

'What is it?' asked Mrs. Cable softly. 'Who is
the offender this time? Do you know?'

Susanna nodded; she had no need to speak, for
Mrs. Cable's ear had already caught the inflection
of a well-known voice.

'Is that Jonathan?' she asked, horrified. 'Has
he got to come in here with his hat on, too? People
will think he has no manners. I suppose Mr. Coffin
went over and told him the story!'

The former scene began to repeat itself. The
marshal, receiving no attention from the minister,
snatched his neat little hat from his head and thrust
it at him.

Mr. Cable's voice carried very well.

'You are a United States officer, I understand?'

'What? Yes, suh.' The marshal was a little
cautious now with these Northerners who talked
back.

'Very well,' said Mr. Cable, 'you are a servant
of ours; you may hold my hat. Don't carry it off,'
he added sharply, and turned away.

'Oh, dear,' sighed Mrs. Cable. 'Jonathan had that all thought up to say before he came over here. What is he doing now?'

'It's all right,' Susanna was able to assure her. 'I think the marshal must be making an apology, and he has given back the hat. The judge was looking around; he was about to rap for order. I must be quiet.'

Jonathan Cable had by this time recognized some friends in the group around Louis's chair. With his hat set firmly on his head, he worked his way through the crowd around the end of the table and up to this group, speaking with great composure to those he passed. He received congratulations from many of these, and several, with meaning smiles, put on their own hats, as if it were a sort of salute to his pluck.

CHAPTER IX

Louis Leaves without Saying Good-bye

JONATHAN CABLE pursued his triumphant, orderly course around the room until he arrived at the position that he preferred, almost directly behind the chair in which the prisoner sat. He looked deliberately this way and that to see if any one yet challenged his right to wear his hat in court; especially his eye dwelt on the marshal, but the marshal was a beaten man; he still stood in the doorway, watching the last comers straggle up the stairs, but he no longer hectored them, and he avoided looking into the court-room at all.

Since there was no question about the hat, Mr. Cable seemed to feel free to remove it, though holding it conspicuously against his chest as if ready to pop it on again in case of difficulty. A moment more and the restless roomful had forgotten the interruption altogether, for the commissioner had begun to read his decision, and a strained attention settled on the crowd.

The Commissioner read very badly; his voice was low, and his face was bent down over his notes. He read on and on and on, reviewing the evidence at great length, while his audience remained painfully attentive, waiting for the important decision to be reached.

Perched up on her rickety chair, Susanna grew very tired; if she moved, the little chair squeaked noisily and half a dozen people looked around at her. Susanna tried to keep her mind on what the judge was saying; but she had as much difficulty with the legal terms as with the low tone.

'If Tristram read like that I'd tell him his mouth was full of mush,' she said to herself. 'I wonder what Louis is thinking!'

Poor Louis! Sitting directly opposite the judge, he could hear better than any one else, and he looked as if he understood the long story. But it must be hard on him, Susanna thought, to be waiting through the flow of words that would almost certainly send him back to slavery. But of course he could not altogether give up hope until the decision was actually given out.

In their eagerness to hear, the crowd pressed up closer to the table. Susanna could see that Louis was being uncomfortably crowded. The Columbus marshal on the one hand, his owner on the other, unconsciously moved their chairs up as those standing behind them pushed against them. Louis looked around and slipped his own chair a little way back to give them more room, smiling at Jonathan Cable as the minister managed to move over to one side.

Did Jonathan Cable wink at Louis? It would seem very unlikely in a man of his dignity, but

Susanna, now alert, felt certain that he had; and that there was meaning in the wink. Louis's expression did not change, but he looked at the men on either side of him and then around the table. All of these were listening intently, eyes on the judge. Louis slipped his chair back a little farther.

No one noticed the movement. Neither Louis's master nor the marshal paid any attention when Louis rose quietly to his feet and slipped around back of his chair.

The judge's even monotone covered whatever slight noise had been made. Jonathan Cable tugged gently at the colored man's sleeve and Louis dared step back again. By this time half a dozen other men of the sympathetic group gathered there had comprehended what was going on. Mr. Cable dexterously tucked his hat into Louis's hand and slipped in front of him, while behind the slave a narrow passage opened itself, just wide enough to let his slight body edge through.

Susanna watched, hardly daring to breathe. Louis went round the end of the table, holding Jonathan Cable's hat up against his shoulder. This was dangerous territory, but he went along slowly, almost apologetically, with the hat up in plain sight to show any one who might be suspicious that he had come in from the outside, and was now leaving his standing-room to some one else. Once he reached the colored people on the other side of the room, he ran less risk of being recognized, but every extra minute added to the danger of some one discovering his absence.

It seemed impossible that neither the marshal nor Louis's master should remain much longer unaware of the empty seat between them, but still they listened and still Louis moved on with great self-possession. He reached the crowded door and passageway, where the marshal stood on guard. The marshal glanced at him as he made his way through the group of Germans there, but he saw only one nigger less to bother with, and wasted no thought on him. Louis disappeared from sight, through the door, and none of those responsible for him or for the conduct of his trial knew that he was no longer in the court-room.

The next five minutes crawled on. Louis had a good start, if he continued to keep his wits about him. He knew Cincinnati streets and some people who might help him; and he had the hat.

Susanna, her cold fists clenched in excitement, was planning out what routes she would take if she were in Louis's place, when she saw the Columbus marshal turn to catch the eye of Louis's master at some statement of the Commissioner, saw him look down absently, and then with growing surprise at the empty space between them, and shoot to his feet.

'The prisoner is gone! Louis is gone, your honor!' he cried frantically.

A few of those looking innocently on knew very well the cause of the disturbance, but most of them were at a loss. They tried to see for themselves what the trouble might be; they shouted questions at the marshal as he struggled round the table; and they blocked the doorway as they tried to join, all at once, in what promised to be a thrilling chase.

Through the hullabaloo the Commissioner rapped on the table and announced, 'Court is adjourned to meet the following Tuesday!'

'What for?' said the tall Kentuckian beside Susanna. 'They'll never find him now!'

'At any rate, that marshal is responsible to the owner for the full value of any nigger he lets escape,' said his friend.

'What does a nigger care for that? Look at that bunch of them grinning! I'd not be surprised if the marshal was bought off. Maybe the judge was in it, too! Who ever heard of an escape from a court-room in broad daylight? It's impossible!'

They went off together, leaving space for Susanna to come down from her observation point, which she did gladly.

'What did happen?' Mrs. Cable was asking. 'Could you see?'

Susanna did not know how much she could safely tell, even to the wife of an abolitionist; and the court-room was, in any case, not a place for repeating what she knew. Fortunately Mr. Cable appeared just then, smiling and polite, hoping they had not been too much fatigued.

'Jonathan,' said his wife with great directness, 'do tell me what happened.'

'Louis got away,' said Mr. Cable innocently. 'Quite remarkable escape, my dear.'

'Yes,' said Mrs. Cable, 'it was. And I shan't ask any more questions. Only, Jonathan, where is your hat? Have you lost it? I should have expected you to hold it fast after all that fuss over it.'

'My hat?' repeated Mr. Cable vaguely. 'Don't I have it? Well, well! We shall have to look for it.'

Mrs. Cable bit her lip.

'Let's be going, Jonathan. Maybe I shall hear the straight of this some day. Susanna, are you ready to come downstairs with us?'

Susanna followed them silently, though her mind was busy enough. She walked home as fast as she could, and spent a hot and sticky, but pleasant afternoon, stirring peach preserve over the stove in the summer kitchen.

Mrs. Rammelsberg was not interested in Louis and asked no questions, and Susanna was glad of that. The good German woman peeled fragrant peaches and measured sugar over them; she covered the tops of the stone jars filled with hot, thick preserves, and all the time she chattered comfortably on, requiring little reply. Susanna had time to think over what she had seen and to decide that she would tell as little about it as if she had seen nothing at all.

Tristram, however, was full of stories at his supper-time. One of the boys had told him that Levi Coffin had had his hat knocked off in the court-room. Billy had said that Louis had escaped from the court-room, although he was chained to the marshal.

'Brother,' advised Susanna, 'I wouldn't repeat that any more. Thee knows I was there. Levi Coffin's hat wasn't knocked off, and Louis didn't even have handcuffs on.'

'Billy said so. Wisht I'd been there,' said Tristram. 'Everybody knows more than me. Did the marshal let him get away on purpose? Somebody said so.'

'The marshal looked to be the most surprised man in the room,' said his sister. 'But, Brother, if I were thee, I wouldn't tell anything I didn't know from seeing it.'

'Well,' Tristram answered hopefully, 'I did see one thing, 'Sanna.'

He paused to balance a large and luscious portion of peach preserve on his hot buttered biscuit, and eyed it with affection.

'I did see one thing.

'Soon as court was over, a whole lot of men came down from the court-room to the store. They laughed and they slapped each other on the back, and they said, "What about it, friend? Have you got a trap-door here to let fugitives down to the Underground Railway?"'

'What did Levi Coffin say to that?'

'Him? Oh, he said, "Yes," just as solemn and he took them over to the cellarway and lifted the door. It's dark down there and it smells like old potatoes. Then they laughed more than ever.

'But I know Louis isn't down there. I looked for him myself, before I came home. Can I tell the boys?'

'No,' said Susanna disappointingly, 'thee'd better not. But thee may tell me whatever thee wants to.'

Tristram lost interest in the subject and took another hot biscuit.

CHAPTER X

Tristram Hears a Secret and Tells It

THE hot weeks of late summer dragged slowly on. Susanna woke one morning with the feeling that nothing ever happened now. The Underground Railway had not claimed her attention for a long time, and she had not enough to think about to keep her happy.

Out under the grape arbor the air was cool and bracing; she spent an hour there picking ripe clusters of the late Isabella grapes, threatened by thirsty bees, and for a time forgot her discontent; but too soon there were no more pink clusters to disentangle from the vines and to lay in the wide basket.

Susanna set them in the cool cellar, tied a handkerchief over her hair, and set out for her next task. Some farmer had sent in word that he would bring in the Rammelsberg winter supply of oats the next day, and Susanna had been directed to take the oldest broom and sweep out the empty oats bin.

'Not just the floor!' said Mrs. Rammelsberg. 'I think it vould be better that you sveep the valls of the bin and the ceiling, too. So many cobvebs!'

The cobwebs were there, and so was the dry chaffy dust that clings to the rough boards of a barn. It fell into Susanna's face and settled around her neck. She sneezed, brushed a floating cobweb from her disgusted nose, and sneezed again.

'Nonsense!' exploded Susanna. 'Perfect nonsense to spend good time sweeping out a barn like this!'

She went on with her dusty work until she had done it thoroughly and was free to go out again into the open air and wash her face and arms in the cold water of the barn pump; but the mischief had been done. She was not quite the same good, obedient hired girl that she had been all summer, and she knew it.

'I don't want to stay here forever, sweeping out barns and cleaning rooms that nobody ever uses,' she told old Whitey, who had come up for a drink. Whitey drank, snorted, and paced contentedly away.

'It's all very well for a horse, but I could do something better, and a lot more interesting.

'I wish I could go to school ——

'I believe I could even be a school-teacher if I could study some more. A good many of the Coffins have taught school. And I *am* a Coffin, no matter what they call me!'

Back in her mind a question popped up: 'What about Tristram?'

Susanna turned and walked slowly back up to the house. Of course there was Tristram; he must be taken care of and sent to school and there was no one but his sister to do it. Susanna would have to go on being a hired girl until Tristram was big enough to take care of himself.

'But I will go to school again,' Susanna promised herself. 'I will, even if I have to wait till I'm an old maid!'

When Tristram came home that evening, she said: 'Brother, I'm going to study with thee when school begins, so I shan't forget what I've already learned. Thee can teach me anything that is new. Isn't thee glad to be going to school?'

Tristram nodded without enthusiasm. 'I'd rather be going to country school.'

'Why, Brother!' Susanna remonstrated. 'Don't thee remember how thee frosted thy feet on that long walk to school? And how Teacher George punished thee by setting thee in the big wood-box? And there was only one teacher for all the classes! There are good schools here in the city!'

'I liked the boys better back in Indiana,' said Tristram. He seemed tired and there were traces of tears under his eyes.

Susanna tried to get him to talk about Louis, a subject that had held his interest for a long time. Since the slave had walked out of the court-room, Susanna had heard no trustworthy reports of him. She had not told what she had seen, and she asked no questions of the few people who would be fairly sure to have information about him.

A week after the trial, however, she had met Mr. Cable driving down the street, and the hat that he lifted as he bowed to her looked to be exactly the same that Louis had carried away from the trial. Somehow that hat had got back to its owner.

Later, Tristram reported that there was a telegram about Louis printed in the paper. Susanna managed to secure a copy of the 'Gazette,' and there, sure enough, was a dispatch from Columbus saying that Louis had passed through the city on the train, bound up-State for Cleveland. At the proper interval another dispatch appeared in the 'Gazette,' telegraphed from Cleveland, and announcing that the slave had taken the boat there for Detroit, next door to Canada.

At this Louis's master had demanded from the Columbus marshal the market value of Louis, which he placed at a thousand dollars, but the marshal would not give up. Tristram heard that he was off again, some one said in disguise, looking for traces of Louis. He was very reluctant to pay over the thousand dollars.

Tristram himself still held a hope that Louis might lie concealed in the cellar of the store, in spite of the fact that he had more than once secretly carried down a lantern to explore the darkest corners, without finding anything more exciting than jars of lard and vinegar barrels.

To-night the boy would not talk of Louis or of

any of the things that ordinarily interested him, and Susanna sent him off to bed early.

It was late when Susanna at last went up to their attic room. Anton Rammelsberg was at home and sufficiently scrubbed and polished to be allowed to go to bed. The house was very quiet.

Susanna was tired, but not sleepy, and for a while she sat on the foot of her low cot bed with her face turned to the great orange autumn moon. The moon would see many countries before it returned the next night. It would shine on the Spanish Californian coast and the gold miners there; it would pass over the Sandwich Islands that the missionary books told about; it would touch Chinese ports and the wide Indian Ocean, and it would come at last above Nantucket Island, from which Susanna's ancestors had sailed in whalers and trading ships to see all these strange countries and oceans for themselves. Presently it had slipped away from the little window, swinging off on its long journey, with Susanna's wistful thoughts following it.

She had supposed Tristram was sound asleep, but as she moved to brush out her hair she heard his voice, 'Sister!' and knew he had been crying.

'What is it, Brother?'

'I can't go to sleep.'

'The moonlight was too bright, maybe, but it's gone now. Is thee well?'

'I'm not ha-appy,' said Tristram.

'What is it, Brother? Tell me.' Susanna knelt on the floor beside his bed and smoothed his tumbled hair.

Tristram found it hard to begin, and even when he was once started the story came slowly.

'I — wanted to know about Louis, 'Sanna. I went down to the cellar yesterday to look for him behind some barrels there. I took a candle. I'd been afraid to look there before, it was so dark back in the corner. And while I was down there I heard somebody coming down the steps, so I scrooged down behind the barrels and put the candle out I didn't want them to find me.

'It was Levi Coffin and Mr. Cable.

'Levi Coffin said, "This will be a safe place. Now what did thee want to tell me, friend?" And Mr. Cable said, "About Louis. Isn't it time we were sending him on?"

'Levi Coffin said, "Is there any s'picion?" and Mr. Cable said, "No, but there is always possibility of ac'dental discovery." I don't know quite what that means, 'Sanna.'

'It means that somebody might happen to stumble on the place where he is hidden, I suppose,' said Susanna patiently.

'Well, Levi Coffin said the place where Louis was hidden was so public that it made the best kind of protection, and Mr. Cable asked how he ever

'WHAT IS IT, BROTHER? TELL ME'

happened to think of it. Mr. Cable said the place
where Louis first went, with the colored people,
wasn't good, of course, and they knew the police
suspected something, even if Louis was dressed in
woman's clothes; but how did Mr. Coffin ever happen to think of this other place?

'He said he supposed because it was so unlikely;
and Mr. Cable said it was pure genius. I don't
know what that means either. Then Mr. Cable
laughed and said, "A committee room in the basement of a popular downtown church! Who would
ever think of looking there for an escaped slave!"
And they both laughed a little, and Levi Coffin said
he hoped Louis had been improved by the sermons
that went on over his head. He said they were the
only entertainment the poor man had.

'Then Mr. Cable said that perhaps it would be
safe to leave Louis in the city for a while longer, but
he thought he had better be taken away at the
first good opportunity. They both thought that
was right.

'So they went back upstairs. And I crawled out
from the barrels and dusted myself.'

'Well,' said Susanna, 'I'm sorry thee eaves-
dropped, but we can keep the secret, thee and I.
We mustn't so much as hint at it, though, because
thee knows the law would send Louis back to jail
and his master would get him after all. And some
people who helped Louis might be punished.
We'll remember, won't we?'

Tristram flopped over suddenly and buried his face in his pillow.

'What's the matter, Brother?' asked Susanna, alarmed.

Tristram only burrowed farther into the feathers.

Susanna took him by one shoulder and turned him over again capably.

'Now thee tell Sister!' she said.

''Sanna, I thought I could keep it a secret, even from thee. And I did. I didn't tell thee last night, when I first knew it, did I? But those boys teased me to-day. They said I was a baby. They said they would tell everybody at school that I was a baby.

'Then I told them that, anyway, I knew something they didn't. They said I was a baby and didn't know anything. And I told them I knew something a lot of big folks would pay money to know. And they laughed. So I told them — where — Louis — is; in a big church downtown!'

'Brother!' Susanna exclaimed. 'No!'

'Yes, I did.'

'But, Tristram —— What did they say?'

'They just laughed some more. Billy said I was seeing things. But just when they went away I heard one of the boys say he wondered if I did know something, after all, because this was Coffin's store and everybody knew Coffin was a nigger-stealer!'

'Oh — dear!' said Susanna, and Tristram buried his head again to escape the reproach in her voice.

Suddenly she sprang to her feet. 'Tristram, when did this happen? When did thee tell the boys?'

'Just before I helped shut up store to-night,' answered the boy faintly.

'Come! Get thy clothes on! We'll find Levi Coffin and tell him and he may be able to save Louis yet. Hurry!'

Tristram sat up.

''Sanna, have we got to tell him? I'd rather die dead!'

'That doesn't make a bit of difference, Brother. Thee must come along. He may want to ask thee some questions. Be as quiet as thee can!'

Tristram had no choice. He slipped softly down the narrow stairs in his stocking feet, following his sister. Susanna hesitated at the foot of the stairs, but not for long. From the bedroom off the best kitchen came alternate snores; first, high and whistling, signaling that Anton Rammelsberg was sleeping soundly, and then one low and long-drawn-out to certify that Mrs. Rammelsberg was also resting peacefully.

'Come on, Tristram,' Susanna whispered; she raised the latch with great care and stepped out into the night.

On the bench under the apple tree they put on

their shoes, and then Susanna took Tristram's hand and hurried him across the dewy grass to the barn. There, carefully, so as not to flutter the chickens, she lifted down her heavy old side-saddle and girthed it round Whitey. Along the green border of the graveled lane she led the old horse, so that her hoofs should make no noise; once out on the road beyond, she led Whitey close beside a stump and made it a stepping-block to the saddle. At her gesture Tristram scrambled up behind her.

'Is thee on, Brother? Hold fast! We can't take time to explain to Mrs. Rammelsberg now. I will tell her in the morning. Now we must hurry!'

Tristram clasped Susanna's waist tightly, knowing what to expect. Whitey's back was broad and comfortable for slow trips, but when she was forced to trot she jolted her riders unmercifully. Susanna spared neither the horse nor themselves; whenever the fat old steed showed signs of slowing down to take the descending slope more easily, she received a sharp thwack from the ends of the reins and indignantly jolted on again. It was neither a comfortable nor a secure ride, but it brought them very soon to Levi Coffin's hitching-rack.

There was only a low night light burning in one room of the big house; Susanna tilted her head to calculate the height of the moon and decided that it must be about eleven o'clock. Well, she would have to wake some one as quietly as she could.

With Tristram's cold hand in hers they went back on tiptoe to the kitchen door. There she knocked softly four times, the knock that she had been taught to use when she met fugitives on the boat from Louisville; and when she had no answer, she knocked again four times, a little louder. At that there was a faint stir upstairs, not enough to be noticed by any one who was not alertly listening. Susanna waited then and in a moment the door opened.

'Come in,' Levi Coffin's familiar voice said softly. Susanna stepped forward into the dark room, steadying Tristram. She stood still while she heard blinds being drawn down at all the windows. Then a lamp was lighted and the kitchen was no longer mysterious; Levi Coffin looked as untroubled and kindly as always, so that even Tristram felt better until he heard his sister launch into explanation of their coming without even waiting for a question.

She said: 'Tristram told the boys around the store this afternoon something he had overheard — that Louis is in the basement of one of the city churches. He didn't tell them which church it was; thee didn't know, did thee, Brother? We came down here just as soon as I found out.'

Levi Coffin set down the lamp, looking older and very serious.

'I must go get Catherine,' he said, and left them abruptly.

When he came back with Aunt Katy, they seemed to have talked the matter over.

'Sit down, Susanna,' she urged considerately. 'Thy brother can lie on this rug. Levi thinks you had better stay here.'

Levi Coffin turned the lamp flame a little lower, watching it absently.

'If the word had got round already,' he said, thinking out loud, 'they would have started looking for Louis earlier this evening and some one would have told me. Now he should be safe at least till daylight. We must get him away before then.

'Susanna, I think thee will have to help get Louis safely up North. Neither thee nor the boy should be around here to be questioned until the storm blows over.

'Catherine will make you comfortable. Try to get some sleep. I will come back as soon as I can and tell you what is to be done.'

He took his hat and went out into the bright moonlight.

CHAPTER XI

Susanna is Made a Conductor on the Underground Railway

TRISTRAM, provided with a pallet by the stove, went to sleep almost at once. Susanna, who had also been given a thick comfort and a pillow on the kitchen floor, felt that she could not possibly sleep, with so many fearful thoughts chasing through her mind. It was with great surprise that she found herself being shaken by the shoulder, and struggled up from a heavy sleep.

'Wake up, my dear child! Wake up!' said Catherine Coffin's soft voice.

Susanna sat up and rubbed her eyes.

'Thee needs a little breakfast before thee goes,' the voice went on. 'Wake thy little brother, too.'

Protesting and limp, Tristram was finally seated at the table and induced to swallow a glass of milk. Susanna, who was not at all hungry, ate obediently what Aunt Katy suggested.

'Levi will be here soon,' said his wife. 'It is not long till dawn. Come upstairs with me, child.'

They came into a little storage and sewing room, and there Catherine Coffin took down from a hook a dress of some soft gray stuff, cut in the simplest Quaker fashion, with plain fitted waist and full straight skirt.

'We thought thee had better travel as the Quaker that thee is. Levi says that no disguise is often the best disguise,' she whispered. 'Here is thy white neckerchief, and here is a gray bonnet. Yes, it fits thee. I will give thee my own gray cashmere shawl.'

When they slipped downstairs again, they found Tristram dozing with his head on the table, while Levi Coffin looked down at him quizzically.

'He will not give away any more secrets so long as he stays asleep,' he commented. 'Poor boy! It was too much for him. He should not have been exposed to the risk. We never involved our own children if we could help it.'

He looked Susanna over with approval.

'Now we must be going. Thee take the lunch Catherine has put up, and a lap-robe. I'll help the boy.' He lifted Tristram gently and carried him outside.

A thick river-mist filled the air and covered the town; no moonlight could pierce its gray blanket. Susanna stumbled down the dark path as well as she could. She did not see, until they were almost upon them, that two vehicles stood waiting in the street: a closed carriage and a curtained spring-wagon that looked as if it might be used to take garden produce to market.

Levi Coffin laid Tristram down on the back seat of the carriage, where he continued to sleep, and turned to Susanna.

'I want thee to drive to Louis's hiding-place, wait there outside for the time that it will take him to come out, and then take the Hamilton Pike out of the city.

'I am taking the pike myself now, a little ahead of thee. Thee may catch up with me. If thee does, drop back and follow, though not too closely. Just keep me in sight. I have a man or two with me, and we are going to feel out the way, in case the road is being watched.

'Now don't be alarmed if we are stopped. There will be no serious difficulty. Keep pushing thy horse on, and we ought to be on top of the hills by daybreak. This mist will help us.

'Now the church ———' he lowered his voice to give her the directions for that.

'We try to foresee emergencies, thee knows,' he went on. 'If there are difficulties, we think it is usually because we have planned poorly. But if anything unexpected should come up — and it sometimes does! — thee will have to use thy own good judgment. Now let us be off! Thee sees thee has thy own horse. I thought thee would be more accustomed to driving her.'

The two vehicles separated, going off on their different ways with what seemed to Susanna enough racket to waken the whole city. Old Whitey ambled along, very willing to pause soon at the side of the church, where Susanna waited.

watching the basement door anxiously. When it seemed to her that she must surely go to look for Louis, without wasting more time, she saw the indistinct figure of a woman coming through the mist from the church, directly to the carriage.

'From Mista' Coffin?' asked a hoarse voice.

Susanna, startled, assented.

'Then I'm your party. Back seat?'

The figure lifted its skirts awkwardly and climbed in.

'Li'l' boy heah? Sho! Sound asleep! I'll take his haid in my lap. Can't git used to these skirts, for all I been wearing 'em, lo, these many weeks; but they'll make a nice soft pillow for his haid.'

'Thee makes a very good woman, Louis,' said Susanna. 'I thought thee was one.'

'Bettah call me Louise,' suggested the hoarse voice. 'I remembahs who I is then.'

With no great enthusiasm the fat old horse settled down to climbing the hills out of Cincinnati. Susanna urged her on northward while the fog clung mercifully about them. They began to meet wagons coming in to the early market, though they were few and far between. No one was going their way as yet; when they finally sighted a wagon going northward, too, it was not hard to recognize it as that which Levi Coffin was driving. They were coming well up out of the lowlands now, leaving the river fog behind them, and could see ahead of

them in the gr_y light of early morning, though the
sun was not yet above the mist. Susanna kept at
the even distance behind it that she had been told
to maintain, and wondered just how it was feeling
out the road.

She was not left long in doubt. Presently the
wagon halted abruptly; as she came closer to it,
she made out the figures of two men standing there
by the roadside, and could see that a hot argument
was going on.

Panic seized the girl for a moment. What was
she supposed to do now? There was no one to tell
her.

Then she straightened her shoulders and lifted
her square Coffin chin. She could depend on herself, if she had no one else to depend on. Perhaps
these men had nothing to do with her. She would
drive straight ahead.

But there was not room for her heavy carriage
to pass the wagon, which stood in the middle of the
road. She was forced to pull up; and when the steel
tires of the carriage wheels no longer crunched on
the pebbles of the road, she could hear clearly the
exasperated voice of the man by the roadside.

'Well, get out your papers, get out your papers!
That's what we're here to see!'

Susanna realized what was happening. These
were officers guarding the road, looking for runaway slaves, and demanding to see the free papers

of any colored person who might come along.
They might be looking for Louis, or it might be an
entirely different fugitive for whom they were
especially searching, but any negro who could not
prove he was free might be grist for their mill.

Levi Coffin seemed to be objecting mildly. His
contention was that Ohio was a free State still, and
that no officer had the right to detain a man who
had not been proved a slave.

'I heard you say all that before,' said the man.
'The longer you hold back the worse it'll be for
you, I can tell you that! Let them niggers git out
their papers if they have any. You've jawed so
doggoned long, *I* don't believe they've got any.'

He glanced back at Susanna.

'Hey, you! Wait a minute! We'll be ready for
you soon.'

Susanna asked plaintively, 'What is the matter?'

The man looked back again. 'It's all right,
ma'am, just wait a minute.' He addressed himself
again to the wagon. 'Will you show them papers
you've talked so much about, or shall I haul you
and the niggers out of the wagon? I bet I'd recognize more than one of them!'

'Show them the papers, boys,' Levi Coffin
ordered, reluctantly. 'I protest that this demand
on free men is not legal, but we will consent for this
time.'

Susanna could see something handed out to the officers, and saw them unfold papers and bend over them in the uncertain light. They consulted each other, seemed against their desires to agree, and flipped the papers back into the wagon.

'Get along,' said the first one. 'Why on earth did you keep us all this time?'

'I should say,' returned Levi Coffin calmly, 'that it was you who kept us.'

He shook the lines over his horse's back and started on, without a look for Susanna.

'Now, ma'am,' said the first officer. The two turned and tramped back to the carriage.

'Sorry, ma'am, but it's my duty to find out who's in every buggy or carriage or wagon that takes this pike out of the city.' The man was trying in a tired way to be polite, Susanna thought, and she was somewhat reassured.

Through her mind flashed Catherine Coffin's words, a little earlier in that strange morning: 'No disguise is often the best disguise.'

'Thee may look and see,' she said to the officer in her best Carolinian drawl. 'That is my brother and a colored servant on the back seat. I'd be obliged if thee wouldn't wake up the little boy. It might frighten him.'

The man peered in. 'Colored mammy? Got her free papers?'

'No,' answered Susanna steadily. 'She has none. She is a slave.'

The man looked up at Susanna curiously, at her bonnet and shawl and neckerchief. 'Thought Quakers didn't keep slaves.'

'We don't. This slave belongs to a man in Kentucky. My cousin arranged for her to drive up into Indiana with me while my brother and I visit there. She will help me with my brother. We have no father or mother,' she added. 'They died back in the South where we came from.'

The officer was completely disarmed.

'Too bad! So you hired her, did you? That was right. A pretty young girl going round the country, she needs help. I think myself you get better service out of the slaves than the free niggers. They know they'll catch it when they go back to their masters if they don't behave.'

He shook his fist in pretended ferocity at the stooped figure on the back seat. 'Well, Aunty, you look out you don't try to give her the slip. Lots of officers like me around. You'd get caught sure! But I bet you're a faithful old soul.

'Well, Miss,' he smiled to Susanna, 'wish they was all as easy to deal with as you. We had a tough customer there just before you. And it turned out all his niggers was free, too. I don't know what he was up to! Thought for a while he was playing some trick; but I reckon he was just a queer one.'

He took his foot from the wheel and stepped back to the grass of the roadside.

'IT'S MY DUTY TO FIND OUT WHO'S IN EVERY BUGGY OR
CARRIAGE OR WAGON THAT TAKES THIS PIKE OUT OF THE CITY'

'That's all, Miss. Pleasant journey to you!'

'Thank thee,' said Susanna politely. Without haste she spoke to Whitey and the horse moved on.

They drove along in silence. After a long interval Susanna heard the hoarse voice behind her say softly: 'They makes you show free papers if you say you're free, but does they make you show any papers to prove you a slave? No, they don't! That's where they get fooled. Always some way to fool 'em.'

'I said thee was a slave,' Susanna remarked.

'Yes, Miss, and they was ready to believe it without any proof. They fooled themselves. They didn't ask whose slave I was, or where were the papers to show he owned me. Just tell them I'm a slave and that's enough. They don't want to believe any darky is free.'

Louis spoke without bitterness, but his earnest voice rose, and Tristram thrashed about, woke and sat up.

'Where am I?' he asked, bewildered.

'Thee's here with Sister,' Susanna answered promptly. 'We're riding out into the country with company.'

Tristram looked up into the dark face, opened his mouth, and shut it again.

'What's your name, li'l' boy?' Louis's hoarse voice was friendly, but Tristram sat back in his corner and did not answer.

'Cat got his tongue?' Louis inquired.

''Sanna, thee tell,' begged Tristram, and Susanna had a shrewd guess as to his trouble: he did not know whether he was still obliged to answer to the name of Hans Rammelsberg.

Susanna made her decision. 'His name is Tristram Coffin,' said she. 'Mine is Susanna Coffin.'

'Hi!' squealed Tristram, to Louis's indulgent surprise.

'Coffin a mighty good name,' said he.

Susanna decided to go farther. 'I want thee to know, Tristram, that it is Louis riding with us. I know thee will keep that secret.'

'Oh, 'Sanna, I will! I won't say a word!' His face shone.

'Thee'd better know it now than find it out at a worse time. I expect thee to help me get Louis safely up North.'

'I can help,' said Tristram proudly; so proudly that Susanna thought it best to take him down a notch.

'Just do what thee is told to, Brother. And don't talk to people!'

'No,' said Tristram, so humbly that his sister felt ashamed.

She knew it was a risk to confide in the boy, but it was a risk that would have to be met sometime in the journey ahead of them, and she was afraid of what might come out if he were suddenly surprised with the information. How far they were to go, or how long the journey would take, she did not know. By this time they had come within sight of the curtained spring-wagon again. Both horses were tiring with the hill-climbing and their progress was slow.

Susanna had plenty of time to think, and she wondered, not for the first time, what Mrs. Rammelsberg would do when she found that both of her charges had disappeared without a word. Would she be frightened or would she take it as one of Susanna's absences on Underground Railway business? Susanna hoped she would understand, but it seemed asking a good deal of Mrs. Rammelsberg to remain cool when a girl, a small boy, and a horse, all were missing from her household without explanation.

At the moment the shelter of the clean and comfortable German house seemed much more desirable than it had the day before. The dry autumn roads were even dustier than the oats bin. Tristram, having eaten his share of the lunch packed for them, was already wishing that he could have some cold milk, and growing tired of sitting still.

Susanna wondered if Mrs. Rammelsberg would want to take her back when she returned. Certainly a hired girl who picked up and went off just as she liked was not a very desirable kind of domestic assistant, no matter how necessary was the errand that called her.

But at least it was true that the errand was necessary. Even if it had not been Tristram's fault that Louis's hiding-place was no longer safe, still she would have felt she must help the hunted man when she was called on. That was the most important thing to be done.

'Get up, Whitey!' commanded Susanna cheerfully.

They were approaching a cross-roads, where the spring-wagon had already stopped. Susanna drew up beside it, and Levi Coffin came over to the carriage-door.

'I see thee passed the examination,' he said to her, smiling, but he asked no questions.

'We are going to take the cross-road to the next pike,' he said. 'Then we will drive back into the city. Thee will go on.

'I have a letter here for thee to take to 'Squire Stubbs at West Elkton, where thee had better stop overnight. He has often sheltered me and my passengers, and I know he will take good care of thee, and recommend thy next stopping-place.

'I expect thee to take Louis as far as my old home at Newport. You should be able to reach that sometime the day after to-morrow if all goes well and you are not delayed. The roads are hard and dry, and you can make good time — at least thirty miles a day.

'After you reach Newport, it will probably be safe for Louis to put on men's clothing again. North of the National Road there is less sympathy for slave-hunters. But thee consult my friend David Willcuts about that at Newport. I have written a little note to him, too.'

Susanna took the letters and stowed them carefully inside her waist.

'I — I will do the best I can,' she said. 'Would thee mind getting word to Mrs. Rammelsberg about Tristram and the horse and me? I didn't stop to wake her up when I came down to thy house last night.'

'Thee didn't?' Levi Coffin was a little disturbed. 'Well, it may be that Katy will have thought of that possibility. We should be back in town before nine o'clock. I will make sure then.

'Now it is time you were moving on. The pike is a plain road to follow. Louis, I wish thee safety. Next year I expect to visit thee in Canada!

'Good-bye, Cousin Susanna. Good-bye, little Tristram Coffin! I will write to you in Newport. Wait there till you hear from me.'

'Good-bye, Cousin Levi Coffin,' said Susanna gratefully, and the two looked at each other with equal respect and liking, as cousins should, even when one is a shrewd, middle-aged man of affairs

and the other a young girl of no worldly importance, and with only the inheritance of a good
name.

The spring-wagon turned down the cross-road
and rattled away; and old Whitey consented to
trot on.

'Now,' said Tristram, with satisfaction, 'we're
off aren't we, 'Sanna? Just us. Nobody else!'

CHAPTER XII

They Escape a Pursuer

SINCE she had come to Cincinnati, Susanna had found out that she and Tristram had made that cold and muddy trip over one of the most used of the Underground Railway routes.

These Quaker families at the 'stations' were known for their hospitality to whites as well as to fleeing blacks, and Folger Coffin felt that he had done very well by his young relatives when he directed the children to them. They were retracing this same road now as far as West Elkton. Instead of mud puddles there was now dust two inches deep in the wheel tracks, and there were leaves where the limbs had been bare, but the way was not so changed that Susanna did not know it.

But old Whitey had not seemed so slow then, even though she was carrying two on her back, and pulling each hoof out of the sticky clay. It was not reasonable to expect much speed from an old plow horse, who had already crossed the mountains from North Carolina, besides doing her full share of heavy farm work, but Susanna did wish that she would bestir herself a little more. It was no use to wish. Whitey had three gaits, a walk suitable to pulling a heavy plow, a slow trot, and, when much prodded, a jolting gallop that would make the most stupid onlooker regard them with suspicion. Susanna devoted herself to keeping the old horse in a trot.

The day wore on to hot afternoon. They came after a while to a little lane wandering off beside a shaded stream, and there they all drank and washed their faces, while Whitey, with her rein loosened, grazed hungrily on the mat of blue-grass. While they rested for a few minutes in the cool shade, well screened from the road, a horseback rider raced by in a dust cloud, like the swift messenger of bad news.

Susanna was uneasy after that. She had let Tristram get down from the carriage before and trot along by the side of it to get the kinks out of his tired legs, so long as the road seemed clear of travelers. Now she was afraid to grant him this exercise, for fear some other rider should come upon them unawares.

'You tired, li'l' boy?' asked Louis thoughtfully. 'I tell you a story. I know lots of stories li'l' boys like. Once 'pon a time ——'

Tristram forgot his cramped legs while he heard the stories Louis's mammy had told him a long time ago, and later tales of Louis's own eventful life. Susanna listened, too, and was less nervous. The dusty miles went by faster.

'Louis,' she said at last joyfully, 'this must be

West Elkton ahead of us. I wish we had stopped here when we came through before, Tristram. Now thee must get out at the first house and ask where 'Squire Stubbs lives.'

The house of 'Squire Stubbs was known to the lazy man who sunned himself at the door of his ramshackle cabin, but he wanted his own curiosity satisfied before he gave directions. What were their names? Where were they going? He got no answers to any of his questions from the stubborn little boy, and finally gave up, jerking his thumb in the direction they were traveling.

'Biggest house up there,' he said, and tilted his chair back against his cabin, studying them ill-temperedly.

'Thee did that very well, Brother,' Susanna praised him. 'Next time we'll inquire at a better-looking place. But this must be the Stubbs house, I think.'

Their welcome at the home of 'Squire Stubbs was quick and understanding.

'We'll take care of you,' the 'Squire assured them. ' We'll take care of you! Never lost a patron of the Railway yet. What you need is a good supper and sleep. We'll wake you early in the morning and get you off again.'

Susanna gratefully let slip her responsibilities. 'Squire Stubbs took Louis with him, chuckling at his feminine array, and Mrs. Stubbs saw that

Tristram was washed and fed. Susanna ate her supper in the room that had been given her, went to bed before sundown, and slept the heavy sleep of the exhausted.

She woke next morning much refreshed, and when she had rubbed her eyes and remembered where she was and what she was doing, she felt quite pleased with herself. She hooked the excellent gray dress together down the front and was pleased with the look of it, too, because she was sure it must make her look much older.

Tristram had also slept well; she found him waiting for her in the neat parlor, sniffing the odor of frying ham that drifted in from the back of the house.

'Louis is out in the kitchen,' he reported enviously. 'I shouldn't wonder if he got his breakfast first.'

'We won't talk about our passenger,' his sister admonished him. 'And thee will get breakfast soon enough. It can't be more than five o'clock.'

'I'm ready right now,' said Tristram. 'I hope he — I mean I hope somebody tells me some more stories to-day.'

Susanna looked up to see their host at the parlor door and her heart sank, for he was evidently troubled. He sat down and balanced his hat on his knee twice before he spoke.

'I don't know just what to do,' he said slowly.

'Things aren't going to be quite so easy as we hoped. We'd better talk it over.

'I'm told there was a man came to town late last night looking for —— ' He jerked his head toward the kitchen, where Louis was supposedly stationed. 'This man's asleep down the road at a neighbor's that gave him lodging. They said they'd try to tell me when he starts out again.

'They say he rode through here from the south, yesterday, looking for —— ' Again he jerked his head sideways. 'But he didn't stop, thinking he would catch up with him on the road. When he did begin to inquire, nobody had seen anything out of the way, so he began to work back, inquiring as he went.

'They say he was suspicious that there'd be a Dutch boy and girl with the slave he was looking for, because they got word about him from the Dutch boy' — Tristram shrank down in his chair — 'and when they went to look for the boy yesterday morning he was gone and so was his sister. This rider gave the name, but my neighbor said it was long and Dutchy and he couldn't remember it.

'Well! What have we got to work on? How did the man miss seeing you yesterday? He says he came up the Hamilton Pike. Who has seen you to get a good sight of your faces?'

'He must have been the man who went by yesterday while we had turned off the road to get a drink,' said Susanna. 'I'm sure that person was in too much of a hurry to see us.

'Then there were two officers that questioned us only a little way outside the city; but they said nothing about Dutch children and they seemed satisfied.

'I don't think any one took special notice of us till we got here. Then Tristram asked the way at a tumbledown old cabin on the edge of town and the man asked a lot of questions. We didn't tell him anything, but he saw as much as he could.'

'Squire Stubbs whistled softly between his teeth. 'I know that man. Nothing to do but tell big stories. There'll be six runaways in the carriage before he tells it twice. Well, this is my way of looking at it:

'You stay here over the day. Don't ask me any questions about' — he jerked his head again — 'and I won't tell you anything. This man will probably find you here, but all you have to do is to tell him who you are, which I can guarantee. Even if I didn't know it, both of you look enough like Coffins to have come straight from old Nantucket.

'Then to-night I can see that the party under discussion is sent on his way, and you can go back to Cincinnati as may be convenient to you.'

He stood up and beamed reassuringly at them; but Susanna rose, too, looking very serious.

'But I must take Louis on,' she said. 'I will

wait till to-night if thee thinks that is best, and then Tristram and I will go on. Levi Coffin told me to take him to Newport. I must do it.'

The man stared at her.

'Pretty rough work for a nice young girl,' he objected mildly. 'I don't see any advantage in your maybe getting mixed up in a fight.'

Susanna did not waver. 'If I am along there isn't so much danger of a fight. People aren't so rough with me as with a man.

'And Tristram and I need to be far enough away so that we shan't be asked too many questions. Tristram does his very best, but they might surprise him into saying something.

'And, besides, Levi Coffin told me to do it, and thee knows he generally has good reasons for his plans.'

'Squire Stubbs shook his head doubtfully over these arguments.

'We sometimes have to change our plans as we go along. We'll talk about it again later.'

He went on out of the room and Susanna did not see him again until he sat down at the head of the breakfast table. Nothing more was said about Louis.

After breakfast Tristram was sent out to play under the trees, and Susanna, at her request, was given an apron and allowed to wipe the dishes. After that she sat in the parlor, like a fine lady, and wished that she had something to do with her hands or occupy her mind.

She was aroused from this undesirable idleness by a roar from Tristram; when she reached the front door she was greeted by the sight of her brother being led toward the house by his ear, and the hand on his ear was that of a stranger.

Susanna flared indignantly. 'What is thee doing to my brother?' she demanded. 'Let loose of him! Tristram, come here!'

At the unexpected sound of her voice, the stranger relaxed his painful grip on Tristram for a moment and the boy jerked loose, and ran for Susanna's protection.

'Wait right here, Tristram,' Susanna told him. She addressed the little man before her in her broadest Southern accent, which excitement was certain to bring on. 'Does thee have anything to say for thy behavior?'

The man seemed to feel it best to take off his hat as he advanced, but his eyes and voice were hard.

'Yeh, I have. I seen this boy out here and I asked him did he know a boy named Hans, and he looked scared and started to run. So I'm going to ask some more questions.'

'Thee would be enough to scare him, without any questions,' said Susanna scornfully.

The man looked up at her from the lower door-step, where he stood.

'Maybe the question would be enough to scare him without me,' he retorted. 'Say, boy, where is Hans? I'll twist your ear again, if you don't give me a civil answer.'

Tristram ducked behind Susanna's skirt .

'Brother,' said she, 'run and find 'Squire Stubbs. Ask him to come here right away. Now,' she turned to the intruder, 'will thee give me thy reason, if thee has any, for frightening a child, so much smaller than thee is, and helpless in thy hands?'

The man measured her with his eyes. 'Come to that, I don't know but what I'm smaller than you, but I'm not complaining about being frightened. I've got nothing to be frightened about. Maybe you have.

'Come on! You tell me, and I won't make any trouble for you. I hear that last night there was a boy and girl drove into town and they had a carriage load of niggers with them. I'm after one of them, named Louis. They asked the way to this house, and they haven't left town yet that anybody knows of.

'The boy and girl has one of these Dutch names — Rammelsberg. They call the boy Hans. These Dutch are all square and chunky and yellow-headed. Most of them got a queer brogue. You see I'd know 'em. Bring 'em out and I'll do the rest!'

Susanna looked at him so long and steadily that the man actually lowered his eyes, though he could still bluster.

'Don't ye try to lie out of it. We can find them without you as well as with you; but there'll be a sight more trouble for you!'

He seemed to shrink a little as 'Squire Stubbs came around the corner of the house, holding Tristram's hand in his own large one.

Susanna spoke first. 'This man is asking if we have a Dutch boy and girl in the house; he mentioned a carriage load of colored people, too. I was about to tell him that Tristram and I were the only young people here.'

'That's right,' said the 'Squire. 'What did they look like?'

'The girl was full-grown; one of these foreign women that work out in the field, they say. Red-faced and chunky. You'd know her by her Dutch brogue, and the boy, too. The boy was just an ordinary boy about town. Worked in the store for Levi Coffin, the great nigger-stealer. We tried to get Coffin tied up with the case, but he was too smart.

'I hear they had several niggers with them, and I'm pretty sure one was the man we're hunting.'

'Squire Stubbs said calmly, 'There was a boy and girl stopped at our gate yesterday afternoon, but they hadn't any carriage load of negroes.'

'Which way were they going?' the man demanded feverishly.

'North. They could have been a good way on by

this time if they kept on at the rate they were going.'

The man began to beat his thigh in vexation.
'How did I miss 'em? I'll get me a fresh horse and
catch up with them yet. If I can get hold of them,
they can tell me something, I'll bet on that!'

He almost ran down the walk, while Susanna
watched him serenely off, her hands folded across
her apron.

'Well,' the 'Squire twinkled at her when the intruder had scurried out of sight down the street,
'I should say it runs in the blood. You make
nearly as good a conductor for the old car, Emancipation, as the President of the Railway himself.'

Susanna permitted her eyes to twinkle back. 'I
thank thee,' she said demurely. 'Now I'm going to
see if thy wife won't let me help bake pies. Tristram, thee'd better play in the back yard for the
rest of the morning.'

'They meant to send me word,' the 'Squire
apologized. 'He must have slipped out unbe-
knownst. At any rate, you handled him so well he
didn't know how well he was side-tracked. See!
There he goes, on his own horse, I reckon. Nobody
in this town wants to hire him one.

'Some of these officers I feel sorry for, but not
him. I only hope he'll get tired enough to take
some of the meanness out of him. Twisting a little
boy's ear!' He felt in his pocket and brought out

a penny for Tristram, who ran off much comforted for his sore ear.

'I don't know what you plan to do with your rig,' the 'Squire said to Susanna in the late afternoon. 'Usually they hire a Cincinnati rig, or borrow one, and the next day the driver takes it back. We forward passengers from here in our own carriage and drive it back ourselves from the next station. I thought you'd be taking this outfit back yourself, but you seem set on that point. Do you go on in it, or leave it here till you come back?'

Susanna considered doubtfully.

'The horse is my own,' she told him. 'She's not a fine animal, but she's about all I have. And I'm right fond of her if she *is* so slow. She brought Tristram and me up from Car'linya. The carriage is Cousin Levi Coffin's old one. Since he didn't give me any other directions, I think I'd better drive on in it and find out what to do with it when I reach Newport.'

'As you say,' the 'Squire assented. 'Just as you say. Now I'm going on to the next station with you.' He waved aside Susanna's protest. 'I wouldn't feel right to let you go on by yourself. I aim to start as soon as it's fairly dusk. Then before the moon rises we'll cut over to the river road where we aren't likely to meet many people, especially this man who is chasing around the country. Though my guess is that he will be fagged out before night.'

'I wouldn't be afraid,' Susanna said with great earnestness.

The 'Squire smiled at her.

'Don't you know that they always send an old conductor out with a new one to teach him the tricks of his trade? You'd better get a nap now, The little boy can sleep to-night.'

The tall, flowery-faced clock was striking seven when he appeared in the parlor, announcing,

'The old car, Emancipation, Number One, is waiting on the track with steam up and freight on board!'

Susanna gathered up her shawl and said good-bye.

'I'm going ahead on my old nag,' said 'Squire Stubbs. 'When we turn off on the river road, I'll tie her to the back of the carriage and drive for you That road is rough going. All aboard!'

He was off at a trot in the growing dusk. Susanna glanced into the back of the carriage to make sure her passenger was really there; without speaking to him she started old Whitey to follow the 'Squire's broad back.

CHAPTER XIII

A Drive through the Night

THROUGH the pleasant twilight Susanna drove silently on. Her eyes grew accustomed to the dark, and usually she could make out the dim figure on horseback ahead of them, but sometimes her imagination played tricks and for a moment she would be afraid to look up, for fear it might be the horse of their pursuer that she would see, instead of the good nag of their friend, 'Squire Stubbs.

The 'Squire turned at last into a side road that was little better than a country lane. When they were well out of hearing of the pike, he dismounted, tied the horse's reins to the back of the carriage, and climbed in beside Susanna.

'Now,' he said, 'I'll drive, while you look out for stumps.'

'Is it a bad road?'

The 'Squire arranged the lines easily, crossed in his big fist, and settled in his seat, leaning a little forward.

'Git up!' said he. 'Bad road? Well, part of it's good enough this dry weather. Corduroy never gets level, the best of times, and nobody ever seems to get round to taking the stumps out. Reckon they'll rot out some day, and save the trouble. But that's all the better for us, because nobody ever travels this road that can take the pike.'

The left front wheel rose abruptly, tilting the carriage well over. Without space for a breath between, the left hind wheel did the same.

'Hold *on!*' said the 'Squire. 'I'd forgot that old stump was there. When the moon comes up, we can see them better. Not that we can miss all of them even then, but it's something to know when they're coming.'

'I know,' Susanna returned, without alarm. 'We came over bad roads a good deal of the way from Car'linya.'

'Old stager, eh?' the 'Squire chuckled. 'Well, there aren't many of us old fellows about that don't know the rough roads from experience, but you youngsters will have better ones. The Underground will have fine level rails twenty years from now.'

'Twenty years!' Susanna exclaimed, dismayed. 'Surely they'll do something about slavery before that!'

'I don't know,' the 'Squire said sadly. 'I don't know! Slavery's old; as old as this country, as old as the world, I guess. When I was young, I used to think I'd live to see it ended; but we're seeing worse times lately, instead of better, what with the Fugitive Slave Law and all.'

'That's why I'm going to Canada this time,' Louis spoke up suddenly. 'I used to think, so long

as I git away from that man's sight and don't do
him no harm, he'll let *me* alone; but I'm not a man
to him, I'm a note on the bank. I'm going to git
so far away he cain't nevah cash me!'

'We'll see that you get there, Louis,' the 'Squire
asserted gently. 'The old Underground is good
enough for that, even if it can't end slavery. By
morning we ought to be near Richmond. I know
plenty of safe men to take you on into Newport,
and we don't often have trouble north of that.'

'Isn't Richmond a station?' asked Susanna.
'There are plenty of Quakers there and Germans,
too.'

'No-o; too public a place, maybe. I don't know
any much-used station right on the National Road.
The little country towns away from main-traveled
roads are the best.'

'What about Cincinnati?'

'Cincinnati don't come under the rule, because
Levi Coffin is a genius. They didn't send many
passengers on before he went down there to open
his free-labor store six-seven years ago. Slaves
would slip across the river and get caught and sent
back because nobody was sharp enough to hide
them. White people didn't want to help; they were
afraid. He has managed to shame a good many of
them into doing what they know is right; and the
Underground is getting more popular, but that is
due to Levi Coffin altogether.'

The 'Squire spoke with feeling, and for a moment Susanna caught his vision of her cousin as a wise and brave and self-forgetting figure.

'Who-oa!' said the 'Squire firmly. 'There, old hoss, see that stump in the middle of the road? Don't fall over it! All right! The axle will scrape as we go over, but no harm done. Now, hold back a little till my nag gets over, too.

'There's the moon to help us,' he said presently, with satisfaction. 'See the crick down through the trees? I like the smell of river roads.'

The carriage swayed down into a dry mud-hole. Old Whitey set her feet well apart and hauled them triumphantly up to the level on the far side.

Susanna chuckled. 'I like the smell of them better than the feel. When I lived at Folger Coffin's up in Indiana, I heard a story about a free colored man who drove up from Car'linya twenty years before, all by himself. Somebody told him that after he left the National Road he must strike down Blue River, and he did — right down the middle of the river-bed. It was low water, of course, and somebody found him pretty soon and persuaded him to come up on the river road. But I never thought he was as stupid as some folks seemed to.'

The 'Squire laughed, too. 'You think the river-bed might be smoother than some river roads. I wouldn't doubt it a minute. I tell you, though, there is one advantage in a road like this: it takes

your mind off your other troubles. Now this
stretch ahead of us is in fair repair. I wouldn't be
surprised if you could snatch a little sleep. The
little boy has been dreaming this long time now.
Wrap up well in your shawl. The night air is getting sharp.'

Susanna obediently followed directions. Not all
the bumping of their slow journey, nor the bright
moon peering down into her face, as if to find what
brought her so far from their last meeting at the
Rammelsbergs, was enough to keep her awake.
She dreamed confusedly, and often woke, but much
of the long night she slept away like a good traveler.

Late in the night they came out onto a much
better road; then, contrarily, Susanna woke broad
awake and did not nap again. Louis and Tristram
slept heavily and the others did not talk. Susanna
watched the moonlit road, but no one peeped out of
the dark houses to see why they rattled by at such
an hour, nor did they meet the rider, the sight of
whom they dreaded.

At early morning they turned back to a farm-
house set well off the road, from whose chimney
smoke was beginning to curl up. Susanna held
tired Whitey's reins while the 'Squire knocked
confidently at the door.

'Station open for Underground passengers?' he
asked as the door opened.

The farmer, standing there with unlaced shoes,

and tousled gray hair, threw the door wider open.

'Any time!' he answered cordially. 'Station master is just getting his uniform on!'

The 'Squire helped out his stiff and sleepy passengers. 'Two chips of the old Coffin block,' he introduced Tristram and Susanna. 'Now this passenger we'll take inside right away. What about it?' He looked Louis up and down, dress, bonnet, veil, and gloves. 'We've been pestered with a visitor at West Elkton — a man after a certain Louis that escaped from trial at Cincinnati. An officer might get the idea that this was the man even in these clothes. Have you seen officers around here? How careful must we be?'

Daniel Clark's lip curled with a faint scorn. 'Little shoo-fly around the neighborhood yesterday, I heard. Wore his horse out running around asking questions, but he didn't find out anything. We didn't know anything to tell, 'far as that goes. He was asking for this Louis, and we said we hadn't seen him; but I don't know whether the man believed us or not.

'Sit down, sit down. Breakfast will be ready before long. You want a horse and carriage, do you? In this note thee shows me, Levi says that the consignment goes on to Newport.'

"The whole outfit goes on together. The horse is tired, but she'll rest up through the day. I counted on your seeing them over to Newport to-night. The girl is a brave one, but I'd feel better if she had an old hand along.'

Daniel Clark said mildly: 'Well, I don't want to shirk, but business on the Underground has been just a leetle heavy lately; and I'm not so young as I used to be. Fact is, I can't be out half the night and make much of a hand on the farm the next day; and I've been out with one load already this week.

'Now I can find some younger man to drive; or I could set them on the way myself as far as the beginning of the Newport Pike, the other side of Richmond. Likely I could pick a ride back from there. The Newport Pike is pretty safe. The toll-gate keepers have instructions to let all Underground cars through free of toll; and they could tell us if any danger was reported. That's what I'd recommend; though I don't look for trouble to me or anybody else.

'And another thing. My judgment is that it would be safe enough to travel in broad daylight. I could start right after a noon dinner.'

'You wouldn't go through Richmond?' inquired the 'Squire with some disapproval.

'No need to do that. We usually bear off north by the mill and miss the main part of town.'

The 'Squire began to feel something of his confidence. 'You ought to know your own territory. I'll leave it with you. Only remember, this case is more ticklish than most.'

The 'Squire rode off after breakfast with hearty good wishes to his companions of the night. He said that they must stop with him as they came back to Cincinnati; he expected that the whole thing would soon blow over and they would be returning in a few days.

Susanna was not so sure of that; but as the day passed and no one came to trouble the quiet house, her confidence also grew. Louis wandered around for a little while in the orchard, while Susanna kept a vigilant eye on the road. Louis had spent the day before in the haymow of a barn not far from the Stubbs'; and the powdered clover leaves still sifted down from his bonnet and veil and out of the gathers of his skirt. It was not a bad place to stay, he said; a haymow was much more like home than a jail; but, he added patiently, he did get tired of keeping still and of wearing dresses. Susanna was glad that it would be only a short time before he would be free to walk around as he liked.

They began the third stage of their journey with the sun at its full height.

'My son-in-law went to town to-day. He said he'd carry me back,' Daniel Clark explained, settling himself with the tired droop of a hard-working, elderly man. 'Does thee want to drive or shall I? All right. Go ahead.'

On the two days before, Susanna had felt herself to be taking part in an adventure; she had great responsibilities and she was in some danger. This hot afternoon her journey was all at once no more thrilling than a trip to town with eggs and butter for market. They came nearer to the little city of Richmond and met more vehicles, but she felt no concern. The drivers spoke to Daniel Clark, looked the unfamiliar horse and carriage over, and passed on, minding their own business.

At the first toll-gate on the Newport Pike, Daniel Clark clambered out of the carriage, his duty done.

'Underground Railway car,' he said to the toll-gate keeper. 'Free, as usual?'

'Free,' the man answered, lifting the bar.

'Safe down the pike to Newport? No suspicious characters?'

'I ain't seen any.'

Daniel Clark reached up a hard brown hand to grasp Susanna's.

'I bid thee farewell, Susanna Coffin. Thee follows the pike now, about eight miles. Thee knows how to pass the toll-gates free, and all thee does in Newport is to ask the way to David Willcuts'. He is the president of this toll-road company.'

He went off stiffly up the road, his errand of mercy discharged, intent on picking up the thread of his ordinary life again. Susanna drove on.

It was nearly dusk when they came in sight of a toll-gate just outside a village that Susanna guessed must be Newport itself; and beside the tiny hut of the gate-keeper stood a horse and rider. For all that she could see the rider might be friend or enemy or neither, but her old fears came back with a rush.

She told herself bravely that she was only startled because she was tired; that she had nothing to fear within sight of the protection of Newport; but still she found herself checking old Whitey as much as she dared, for which the old horse was entirely willing.

As she came up to the toll-gate, the rider was just lifting his horse's reins after a final word with the old keeper. Susanna shot one glance at his face as the horse moved off; she caught her breath in astonishment, and cried after him,

'Jack! Jack Fairfield!'

The tall rider half-turned in his saddle, but his questioning face showed no recognition, and he was soon out of hearing.

Susanna's eyes stung with tears. It would have been comforting, she thought, to see an old friend again; but perhaps Jack Fairfield had forgotten her.

The toll-gate keeper was deaf, and he was new to his position. Susanna had no time to give way to a wave of loneliness; instead she was obliged to lift up her voice and shriek at the old man that she was on business for the Underground.

'Never heard of it,' the toll-gate keeper shook his head, and held out his hand.

'Did thee ever — hear — of — Levi — Coffin?' asked Susanna.

'Hey? Coffin? You some of his folks? Yes, I heard of him. Everybody's heard of him, even where I come from. This town of Newport, they think the sun rises and sets in him. You want to come through free, is that it? Well, drive on. Proud to have seen ye.'

Susanna did not try to extract directions from the deaf man for reaching David Willcuts' house. Instead she drove slowly up the one long street of the village, looking for some one to whom she might speak without leaving the carriage. There were lights in the kitchen windows, and all Newport seemed to be eating its supper. Susanna was hungry too, and she knew that Tristram must feel starved.

She pulled Whitey to a halt by the first person they met, a man rambling aimlessly along the little beaten path through the grass of the roadside.

'Will thee tell me where David Willcuts lives?'

The man growled in his throat something that could not be understood. Then he seemed to remember his manners, for he removed his broad-brimmed beaver hat, and answered in a peculiar, mincing tone,

'Thou doesn't know that I am a stranger in the town. They can give directions to — thee at that store up the street.'

Tristram meditated softly as they drove on. 'That was a funny Quaker. I never heard one talk like that before. I guess he was a new one.'

Susanna said: 'He was funny. It seemed to me I had seen him before. Some of his Quaker relatives, I suppose. Or it may have been imagination and the dark.

'And I thought we met Jack Fairfield back there by the toll-gate; but I'm not sure now who it was.'

'We all seeing things to-night,' said Louis mournfully. 'Seem to me I know that last man's voice well, but I can't place it. I've listened to so many voices while I been hid one place and another. To-morrow I may remember whose this was like; I hope I don't dream about it. Most of the voices I heard I don't never want to hear again in this world.'

Tristram shivered, and Susanna leaned out and looked back after the figure disappearing in the darkness, which had brought this queer feeling to them all; but there seemed nothing unusual about it.

David Willcuts' house proved easy to find, and Susanna, with her note of introduction, was cordially welcomed.

'I'm sorry we can't take you in,' said Levi Coffin's friend. 'My own house is pretty well full to-night with visiting relatives. We could give you pallets on the floor, but you would not be comfortable. I'll take you over to Levi Coffin's old house, where I know there is plenty of room; most of the family is away to-day. They can give you supper and beds. I'll make arrangements for taking thy passenger on myself.'

He walked back down the road beside them, making keen inquiry about their journey up from Cincinnati.

'You came through well, considering how badly they want this man. We have seen nothing of thy horseback rider here. The slave-hunters have about stopped hoping to find out anything in this town.

'Here we are. Drive into the side yard. The barn is just ahead.'

He brought them to a stop beside a reassuringly square and solid brick house.

'Wait till I knock.'

The kitchen door opened quickly; Susanna could see him talking with a colored woman who sheltered a candle flame with her hand.

'It's all right,' he said, when he came back. 'Get out and come in. The whole family went down to Richmond and expected to stay to meeting in the morning. But their housekeeper, Nancy, will take care of you and be glad to do it.'

He led old Whitey and the carriage down the grassy slope to the barn, and the tired party thankfully found themselves in a big warm kitchen, so large that it was used also for dining-room and general work-room.

David Willcuts returned, rubbing his hands with satisfaction. He saw that Nancy, quiet and capable, was putting together a quick supper for the travelers, that she had given them hot water for washing, and set their chairs where neither the fireplace flame nor the candle-light would shine too brightly on their faces, though the blinds were drawn down.

He looked with amusement at Louis, who, still afraid to remove his bonnet, was having difficulty in not washing his veil as well as his face.

'I'll send around a man's suit for thee right away,' he said to Louis. 'Thee will feel more at home in it. Just keep quiet and out of sight now, and we'll have thee through in no time. I'll take thee on up to Randolph County to-morrow after meeting. There is a good Underground station now at Cabin Creek. New man in the neighborhood who is a great help. From the South, too, like some of the rest of us.

'Good-bye, my friends, sleep well. Nancy, I am obliged to thee for taking them in. Why doesn't thee tell them the history of the house if they are not too tired?'

Nancy beamed.

'Mist' Willcuts knows I like to tell stories about this house,' she said when they were by themselves. 'I stayed here all the first winter after I came to the North, while Mist' Coffin wrote letters and sent money down South for me to pay for myself. I had the money to pay for my freedom, but I was afraid they would keep me and the money, too, if they knew about it. So I ran away.

'I stayed in cornfields by day and traveled by night, and sometimes I hadn't anything to eat but green corn and berries. Everybody said if I could get to Newport I would be safe with Mist' Coffin, and I was. I hope he and Mis' Coffin are well? I pray for them every day.'

'They are well, thank thee,' said Susanna. 'I don't think either of them has time to be sick. Has thee been here ever since thee came North?'

'I went to the Friends' School up in Randolph County,' Nancy answered proudly. 'I can read my Bible and write as well as any one. I married there, too, and lived in the settlement at Cabin Creek. But my husband died this winter, and I was glad to come back to this house to work. No matter who rents it — and they are nice folks — it always seems like Mr. Coffin's home to me, and I keep hoping they will come back some day.'

'You feel safe here?' Louis asked earnestly.

'Let me tell you,' said Nancy impressively. 'More than two thousand slaves have been sent on from this house, and none of them were ever caught! The Lord watches it!'

Louis sighed and went back to his apple pie. 'Maybe I'll feel safe after I get to Canada,' he said, though not too hopefully.

Much good food had refreshed Tristram. 'Susanna,' he ventured, 'can I ask her how they hid the runaways?'

Susanna looked questioningly at the brown woman. 'Maybe thee doesn't want to tell?'

Nancy laughed. 'They never had to do much hiding. The officers were afraid of Mist' Coffin. He had more than one arrested for kidnaping, and they never dared to come into his house. I did hear once that Mrs. Coffin thought the house might be searched and she put two young slave girls in bed with a feather tick on top of them; but they giggled so much that she had to take one girl out and put her into another bed. But that was a false alarm.

'Myself, I think this old cellarway would be a good place. It is so steep that you have to watch careful as you go down. If you press hard to the left at the bottom of the stairs, you push open the door of a little storage closet there; but if you didn't know it you'd never find it; you'd be watching that you didn't fall off the steps in the dark.'

She checked herself suddenly. 'Somebody knocking at the front door. I wonder who, this time of night. Maybe Mist' Willcuts sent somebody with the clothes. No, they would have come to the side door. You go right on with your supper. I'll shut the door between this room and the parlor.'

It seemed a long time that she was gone. The fire in the fireplace was burning low, and Susanna did not make bold to replenish it. When Nancy came back, she shut the door sharply behind her; even in the shadows Susanna could see that she was sobered.

'There's a queer sort of man in there, says he wants to see Levi Coffin's grandchildren. Says the toll-gate keeper said they drove in to-night. I couldn't get rid of him, and I'm afraid you'll have to see him or he'll sit there till morning. I won't light a fire for him.'

She looked at Louis, considering. 'I'll take you up these back stairs right now before I wash the dishes. When Mist' Willcuts sends the clothes I'll put them at your door. The little boy can sit by the fire till his sister comes back.'

Susanna, tired and reluctant, settled Tristram in a big rocker and went in to see her caller.

CHAPTER XIV

Jack Fairfield Tells his Own Story

NANCY had left the caller in the cold parlor with only a single inhospitable tallow candle on the mantelpiece, but the man showed no signs of understanding that he was not desired to stay. He came forward effusively, holding out his pale hand. His clothes were the plain clothes of an orthodox Quaker, with straight-collared coat and wide-brimmed beaver hat, but his words had a twist that was most peculiar to Susanna.

'I didn't know it wert thou, when I sawest thou this evening,' he smiled, and again the girl had an unhappy sense of having seen him before. Where was it?

'I don't know thy name,' Susanna answered quietly, stepping back from him.

'Thou wouldest not remember it,' the man said, still as agreeably as he could. 'But I am well-known to thy grandfather, Levi Coffin of Cincinnati.'

'Levi Coffin is not my grandfather.'

'Great-uncle, of course. I make these mistakes, thee knowest. But any Coffin is a friend of mine for the sake of that great abolitionist.' He seemed to study the effect of his declaration with some disappointment. Suspicion was growing in Susanna's mind; she made no answer.

The girl's silence seemed to bother him. He began afresh.

'I dropped in to ask what kind of a journey you — thou — haddest. Any troubles? Let's us sit down and talk awhile.'

'We thought we did very well,' answered Susanna. She remained standing by her chair, and the man hastily rose again.

'Your — thy passengers? Diddest they come through without any interference?' He smiled knowingly at her. 'It is safe to tell me anything in confidence. I know a great many Underground secrets.'

'My little brother is tired to-night and so am I,' said Susanna evenly. 'May I ask thee to excuse me? If thee comes to meeting in the morning I may see thee there.'

'Close-mouthed, eh? That's all right, but don't be afraid of me.' He came nearer. 'If that woman would give us some coals to light a fire we could sit here and rest and chat. It might be worthest thy while.' He smiled again the knowing smile.

The door opened behind Susanna and they saw Nancy standing there severely, candle in hand.

'I will bid thee good-night,' said Susanna. 'Nancy, will thee open the door for our visitor?'

The man regarded them with narrowed eyelids.

'Good-night, then, since both of thou seem to insist,' he said. 'But let me save thou trouble by going out through the kitchen.'

Nancy sailed with dignity through the room, her arm with the candle extended wide as if she were shooing the unwelcome visitor out.

'I am still able to open the front door,' she said, and before her advance the man fell back reluctantly into the hall and could do nothing but walk down the front steps into the street. Nancy stood at the door, shading her candle, until he had moved off some distance, looking back over his shoulder now and then.

When she turned back to Susanna, the door shut safely behind her, her brown face wore a discreet smile.

'Come out by the fire, Miss. Something there for you to see.'

Susanna felt that she had already seen enough for the day.

'Nancy,' she said, 'I don't like that man. He isn't a Quaker. He was spying.'

'We saw more of him than he did of us,' Nancy answered confidently. 'Don't worry, Miss. This house is a safe place and Newport is a safe town. There! Look at that!'

Susanna's blue eyes rested wonderingly on the tall figure standing before the kitchen fireplace.

'Louis says we are all seeing things to-night,' she

observed faintly. She sat down abruptly in a big wooden rocking-chair and found herself sobbing against its high back.

'I thought — I thought we met thee this evening — on the road,' was all that she could manage to say.

Jack Fairfield was across the room, patting Susanna's cold hand, touching her bright hair softly.

'There! There! I didn't want to scare you, Susanna! Bless your heart, don't cry, girl!'

He turned her gently around to the firelight.

'Look here! Are you a Coffin or are you really a Rumpelstiltskin, or whatever the name is? No Coffin would cry like that!'

Susanna smiled up at him and wiped her wet eyes.

'I thought so,' he said triumphantly. 'A Coffin chin never quivers! I did guess your name right, didn't I?'

Susanna repeated quaveringly, 'But I thought we met thee this evening.'

The young man seemed content. He found himself a low chair and pulled it over beside Susanna. As he started to speak a hard cough got the better of his voice; when it was quiet, he still sat silent, his handsome face grave.

'I suppose you did meet me,' he went on finally. 'You must have called to me, though I didn't realize it at the time. But the farther away from

Newport I rode, the more I heard a voice in my ears, and the more it sounded like yours. I got an idea that you might be needing my help. You did once, on the boat, you know. Anyway, I turned around and came back here. I thought that if I didn't find you, I could stop here at the Coffin house; it would be good for me before I was off at my wild ways again.'

The cough seized him again, and with alarm Susanna watched it shaking him.

'Nancy, couldn't thee get him a hot drink?' she asked.

Jack took the hot cup gratefully. 'Peppermint tea? This is luxury. I like to be coddled.'

The big room was very peaceful. Tristram slept where Nancy had laid him on a rug by the side of the fireplace, and Susanna had no heart to waken him and put him to bed.

'I wanted to see you, too, Miss Susanna, whether you needed me or not. I planned to look for you in Cincinnati before I crossed the river again. I never want to see Friend Levi before I start on these excursions, though I do come around after everything is over to be scolded and washed and clothed and petted. I do like coddling — between-times.'

'What is thee planning to do?' Susanna asked quickly.

He smiled with mischief. 'I'd better not tell. You might argue me out of it. A Quaker can be so reasonable! Let us talk instead about what I have just been doing; for I have been very good, Miss Susanna. Very, very good, indeed!'

He must have found surprise in Susanna's face, for he laughed outright until the cough checked him again.

'You will be more astonished when I tell you. I have been keeping store, just like Friend Levi.

'When I was ill last winter, after that inconvenient time in jail, the President of our favorite Railway came to see me. He pointed out to me that I was always getting into trouble, and that I might expect to continue to be cold and wet and sick rather often if I continued these raids into the South.

'He also told me that it was very wrong of me to go around stealing horses and skiffs, and teaching slaves to shoot up their dear overseers and the benevolent patrollers; but I cannot say that argument made much impression on me. I have known too many overseers and patrollers.

'And then he asked me to consider his own polite and amiable methods of increasing the colored population of Canada. He said that he had sent many more slaves on their way rejoicing than I had, and was likely to send still more; whereas I might at any time stop an angry slave-holder's bullet and there would be an end to my usefulness!'

'I was too contrary to take his advice at once,

Miss Susanna. I am naturally wicked, you see. I had to even up my score with Kentucky first. And I did that. I got a slave through to freedom for every day I had spent in their freezing, dirty jail. It didn't take me long; you may remember that I used wholesale methods.

'Then I set to work to be good. I came up here to Cabin Creek. That's a settlement not far north of here, where there are a lot of colored families. I met Nancy there.' He smiled his flashing smile at the brown woman and she looked over at him with admiring affection.

'I set up a free-labor store there, and I had a little house of my own, and everything was very snug and cozy. Sometimes I drove a fugitive on to the next station after night. Perfectly safe. Nobody ever lifted a finger to stop us. I used to go to sleep driving, I was so bored, and the slave would have to wake me up when we got there.'

He paused and stared absently at the rug.

'What is the matter?' asked Susanna. 'Thee speaks as if thee were not going on with the store.'

He straightened himself with a look of bitter amusement. 'Quite right. I'm not. I couldn't stand it. Measuring off yards of calico and weighing flour and meat!'

'Somebody needed the calico for a dress, and the meat and flour for food,' said Susanna timidly.

'Yes,' said the young man. 'Yes. Of course. I know that.'

He turned toward her, speaking more earnestly, as if he must make her understand.

'Don't you remember, Susanna, that I told you once I was born in the wrong time? The kind of adventurous living I need would have been the natural thing sometimes; but not now. I'm an outlaw. I can see that Friend Levi may be right, but I can't walk his quiet path.'

He hesitated.

'I want to tell you how I was convinced. I — I haven't told you the whole story yet. I thought when I came up here that I would change myself completely. I thought I would learn to be a Quaker. Don't laugh at me!'

'I'm not laughing,' said Susanna. 'I'm — I'm trying not to cry!'

'Well, it isn't worth tears, either,' he said, touched. 'You can see that I didn't succeed. But for a good long time I practiced "thee" and "thou" to myself and I read the Discipline of the Society and tried to live up to all the advices in it. And I thought — I thought I might find a Quaker girl who would marry me and help me to be good,' he finished, humbly.

Susanna could say nothing.

'Well, this week I saw what a fool I was making of myself,' he went on with bitterness. 'An old codger came up to Cabin Creek; drab coat, broadbrim to the life. He came snooping round, trying to talk like a Quaker. I made slips, Susanna, but not such bad ones, I hope. It turned out that he was playing Quaker to see if he could get news of an escaped slave. He made up to me; said he could see that I was a Southern gentleman, though in reduced circumstances, and he could help me if I would help him. Offered me money to find out where this slave was. Said he was the marshal, and the slave had escaped from his custody, and he would have to make good his value. I couldn't fool even that man! I made up my mind that I would stop trying to impose myself on Quakers. I wasn't their sort; anybody could see it.'

'Jack!' Susanna put out her hand. 'Jack! That was the man who came here this evening! Was he hunting for Louis?'

The young man looked up, startled. 'You don't have Louis with you? It never occurred to me that Friend Levi would send his most innocent lambs to guard a man who is being hunted through three States. I — I wanted so much to tell you about myself that I didn't think of you at all, I'm afraid.'

'It doesn't matter,' said Susanna. 'But I know now where I saw that man. I saw him at Louis's trial; he is the Columbus marshal who was responsible for Louis. Louis thought he remembered the voice, but he couldn't think whose voice it was.'

'What did he find out?'

'Only that I am a Coffin. The toll-gate keeper told him that.'

Jack Fairfield stood up and began to pace the floor restlessly.

'My impulse would be to cart Louis on to-night from under his nose. I suppose that you and Friend Levi Coffin would be inclined to leave him comfortably here until the marshal in sheep's clothing loses interest and departs for better hunting elsewhere. But he may hang round for some time. My guess is that he has just come and will stay as long as he thinks that he is taken for a Quaker.'

Susanna said firmly: 'I do think that Louis had better stay. That man may be watching the house to-night. And, besides, Louis and I are tired and so is the horse.'

Jack Fairfield laughed.

'Were you thinking that I would let *you* drive him on? No, thank you. I'll see that you don't run any more such risks. I shall tell Levi Coffin what I think of him for sending a girl off on this desperate errand. But I can easily find another horse and escort Louis myself.'

'Thy cough is a risk in this night air — more risk than any I have run,' said Susanna heatedly. 'Sit down and let me give thee some more tea.'

He yielded to her determination. 'I did promise that I would be good for one more night, didn't I? Of course it's because I want the tea!'

Over his steaming cup he mused, 'You seem to be paid very stingily for all your goodness. You help the poor and distressed and hunted, and all your reward is that you are out in the cold world yourself.'

'I haven't done it for reward, thee knows,' the girl said quietly. 'Thee knows that.'

'Yes, I know it,' he answered, more cheerfully. 'And, more than that, I think your reward may come some day.'

Nancy left the window, where she had been standing for a while, looking out through the narrow crack at the edge of the blind.

'Is it time to go to bed?' Susanna asked her. 'We are keeping thee up late, Nancy.'

Nancy said: 'That man that came here to-night, he's been standing across the road watching the house. I didn't tell you, because I couldn't see that he was doing any harm. But a man rode up on horseback a minute ago and stopped to talk to him, and now they are coming over this way together.'

As she spoke, they heard the trampling of a horse's hoofs, brought to a stop at the side door, the sound of a rider alighting on the gravel, and then a loud double knock at the door.

CHAPTER XV

They are Discovered

BEFORE there was time to open the door, the knocking was repeated, and louder.

'Hello, the house! Hello, the house!' There was no mistaking that disagreeable voice.

'It's the officer who was looking for Tristram and me down at West Elkton,' whispered Susanna.

'Let me attend to him,' Jack said grimly. He took a long stride toward the door, his hand at his belt.

'Jack! Jack Fairfield!' Susanna was in deadly earnest. 'Put up thy gun! Thee promised to be good to-night!'

The man looked down at her in amazement. 'You don't know what this may be like, Susanna. Go into the parlor and shut the door, or run upstairs till I'm through with them.'

The latch rattled in the unlocked door.

'I shall not,' said Susanna clearly. '*Thee promised.*' She slipped in front of him, and stood in the doorway as the door swung open. For a moment the two on the stone doorstep fell back before the tall girl standing in their path.

Then the smaller one said: 'Come on, Marshal. Watch your gun. Tote it handy. Let's get this over with in a hurry.'

'Do you want to come in?' asked Susanna.

'Now what do you think?' queried the little man, advancing into the big dim kitchen. His drab-coated companion followed him, blinking. He seemed to feel still less at ease as his eye rested on Jack Fairfield, whose coat-sleeve Susanna was holding with determination.

'How — art — is ——' he began, with some feeble hope that he might yet put matters on a friendly basis; but the little man cut in on his halting speech.

He had seen Tristram struggling awake, frightened; he measured Susanna with a glance of complete recognition; and in compliment to Jack Fairfield he shifted his revolver to a still more conspicuous position.

'Now,' he said, 'we'll get down to business. I don't care, young lady, whether your name is Coffin or Schmidt or Hey-diddle-diddle; but me and the marshal have compared notes and we are betting you have Louis with you. And I can tell you that you don't get away from me again, no matter how slick you are. We're going to have that nigger. Will you fetch him out, or shall we get him?'

'Does thee have a writ?' asked Susanna.

'I have one, and the marshal has one. We won't take time to bother about them now. Where is the nigger?'

'I think,' said Susanna, 'that you will have to look for him.'

'All right, all right.' The man's voice was cruel. 'Just as you say. But we'll make him pay for this when we get him.

'Marshal, you stay downstairs where you can watch the doors. This young feller will put down his gun and keep you company. The rest of you go along with me and help me look. Hey, you, woman! Get a candle!'

Jack Fairfield's face was a mask as he dropped his revolver on the kitchen table. He watched Susanna curiously as she and Nancy went off into the parlor in front of the little man, who led Tristram on tiptoe by his ear, as if he enjoyed hurting the boy.

Through the first floor of the house they made slow progress. The little man seemed to have planned to make the others do his searching, but he could not make up his mind to trust them, and it was he who examined all the built-in presses, sounded the broad chimneys for hiding-places, and peered into the darkness behind doors. Nancy held the candle as she was roughly directed. Susanna merely accompanied them, encouraging Tristram silently.

'Nothing here that I can see,' the man said as he finished the round of the parlors and hall. 'I wouldn't expect him down here. The attic, now, that's the place for him!'

The four of them climbed the steep, stiffly bannistered front stairway. Just beyond it on the second floor ladder-like steps ascended to the trap-door that opened into the attic.

The little man peered up at them disgustedly.

'Taking a pack of women around!' he complained. 'Well, it can't be helped. Go ahead, you! I'll follow, and you can be sure my gun is ready in case of any nonsense.'

Nancy pulled the rope that opened the trap-door, and one after the other they climbed the ladder. Here the little man evidently had high hopes of running down his victim. He looked behind old chairs and chests, and even sharply around a tall spinning-wheel, and he pounced eagerly on a roll of wheat sacks, lying beside the chimney. Nancy held the candle at arm's length for him as he stooped over in the dusty eaves. Her mouth twitched with scorn as he bumped his head on the low rafters, swore at the pain and dived into a fresh shadow. Now and again he waved the revolver threateningly, but it was plain that his mind was more on his search now than on his companions.

Susanna had come thus far without any definite plan in her mind for Louis; now she thought she saw her chance. She stood near the trap-door, with Tristram close by, rubbing his abused ear. As the man straightened himself once more, receiving a wicked crack on his head from the stout roof-timber above him, Susanna swung Tristram in both strong arms directly over the opening and set his feet on a step well below.

'Tell Louis,' she whispered, before the man had stopped swearing at his hurts, and dropped the trap-door as quickly as she dared over Tristram's head.

'What the —— Is that the nigger?' the little man shouted, and fired senselessly. The candle that Nancy held was snuffed out, and Susanna felt a shock and a queer stinging up her left arm.

The man was stumbling furiously toward her through the dark.

'Open that trap, you!'

'Stay back, then, so thee won't fall through it,' advised Susanna.

'You little devil!' he sputtered, but he halted while Susanna fumbled for the rope and lifted the door.

Down the ladder he tumbled in the faint light that the moon sent through the deep-set hall window. At the foot he controlled himself enough to listen; at a faint sound of breathing from the back bedroom he rushed on. Susanna and Nancy came up with him as he had just caught himself from falling down the step that led from the front bedroom into the room over the kitchen. He paused again.

'There you are!' he said, with cruel satisfaction.

'Breathing hard! Scared, ain't you? Good reason why!'

He waved an arm back at Nancy. 'Gimme the candle! I got matches; we'll light up and see what we see!'

He struck a match, evidently proud to be carrying such a new-fangled convenience, and looked eagerly around. Against the wall stood Tristram, his eyes pleadingly on his sister. There was no one else in the room and the beds had not been touched. To the little man's frenzied ransacking the closet yielded only a variety of women's clothes.

Susanna's arm had begun to throb; she held her handkerchief tightly against it and presently the cloth was wet to the touch; but she forgot the pain as she saw the little man dart at Tristram, seize his wrist and twist it backward.

'You little rat!' said he. 'Now tell me where he went!'

Tears came to Tristram's eyes and he tried to pull away.

'I don't know,' he said, and Susanna knew he was telling the truth. 'And,' he went on bravely, 'I wouldn't tell you if I did!'

'You wouldn't? We'll see!' He brought more force to bear, and Tristram gave a little cry.

'Stop that!' ordered Susanna. The pain in her own arm was as nothing. She wrested Tristram from the vicious grip and put the boy behind her.

'Thee may have a legal right to search this house, but thee has no right to injure the people in it!'

The little man looked up at her and shifted his revolver uncertainly. Something on his hand caught his attention; he saw the dark wet smear where Susanna had forced open his fingers, and then he saw the stained handkerchief against her sleeve.

He turned away in nervous haste and plunged down the narrow enclosed stairway that led down through the kitchen and on into the cellar.

'Come on,' he called over his shoulder, in a tone he meant to make as bullying as before, but without all of his former confidence.

Nancy went on down behind him, Tristram next, and Susanna last, a little dizzily.

'Nothing yet,' he announced in the kitchen. 'Marshal, I've got too many of them. Keep an eye on the girl and the boy while the nigger woman lights me to the cellar. He's sure to be there.'

For the first time Nancy spoke up. 'I can't give you a good light down there. The stairs are too narrow. You'll fall unless you carry your own light.'

'Blast it! Give me the candle, then. Take all three of them, Marshal.'

Susanna found a chair by the kitchen table; she sat there holding her injured arm under the table, wondering what Catherine Coffin would think of all this blood on her nice dress, wondering why Jack looked at her so queerly, and what that unexpected crash in the cellarway might be. Then she laid her head on the table and the room turned black.

The darkness was very comfortable; when she woke, lying flat on her back on the hard floor, she shut her eyes again, hoping to escape from the confusion around her; but Nancy was bathing her forehead with water so cold that she could not help coming back to full consciousness.

The little man was shouting: 'Blast 'em! They set a trap on the stairs to trip me and kill me! I know they did! We'll burn the house down before we leave it without that nigger!' There was a rapidly swelling bruise above his right eye and he rubbed his elbow tenderly.

Susanna heard the voice of the Columbus marshal cut with authority across the raving of his companion. 'I tell you I'm through with this. Come on before you lay yourself liable to a charge of murder!

'It was bad enough running around the country diked out in these clothes and trying to get the Quaker lingo. I felt like a fool and a sneak. But I didn't hurt anybody, and I won't conspire with a crazy man to shoot up women and children. I'm an officer of the law and I don't forget it. Come on before I arrest you!'

The little man gasped and grew purple. 'Scared, eh?'

'It's you that have reason to be scared,' the marshal answered. 'I think, myself, that there's more than an even chance Louis ain't in the house at all. You were so set he was, but you haven't found him!

'And I tell you this: I'm a poor man, and I can't afford to lose a thousand dollars, but neither can I afford to be mixed up in doings like this. I'm going back home and see if I can't compromise with Louis's owner. Maybe he'll knock off three or four hundred.'

He turned to Jack Fairfield.

'Sir, I apologize. I know I don't stand well in your eyes. Your gun I'll leave out under the hitching-rack. You had good sense not to use it; I was ready for resistance.

'Now,' the marshal swung round to the protesting little man, 'we leave town together to-night, to be sure you don't get either of us into more trouble.' And he led him out of the door with a none too gentle hand on his bruised elbow.

Susanna lay very still and limp on the floor, uncertain whether this were a dream or not. If it were really a dream, then it was happily ended by the sounds of a horse's hoofs moving away outside; but the pain in her arm was too real for a dream.

She opened her eyes to see Jack Fairfield kneeling

beside her; with his sharp knife he gently slit up the
stuff of her sleeve and laid it back.

'Flesh wound,' he said to Nancy, hovering over
them. 'Painful, but I don't think it's serious if it's
dressed properly. I've dressed worse wounds than
this when I had to, but I don't trust myself with
her. Go get Dr. Way, will you, please?'

Susanna heard the door close behind Nancy.
Tristram crept up and took his sister's uninjured
hand tight in his. Jack had arranged a tourniquet
and sat on the other side of her, holding it in place.

'But where was — Louis?' asked Susanna
faintly.

'Haven't you guessed?' Jack laughed. 'Here,
boy, hold this stick steady for a little while. I'll
find him, I warrant, and the sight will do your
sister good.'

She heard his feet cautiously taking the cellar
steps, and then a chuckle. Two pairs of feet came
up the stairs, and Susanna opened her heavy
eyes to see Louis before her — but a different
Louis, properly attired in coat and trousers, and
more independent and less fearful.

'You bad hurt, Missy?' he asked, with real
concern. 'I felt this was going to be my bad night,
but it was you that took the worst of it.'

'Louis,' said Susanna, 'where was thee?'

The fugitive smiled apologetically.

'Seemed like I was so used to sleeping in out-of-the-way places that I didn't feel good to sleep in a real bed and a real bedroom. I felt queer when I looked at that feather bed. Well, Nancy had took me up these clothes while you was out of the room, Miss, so I put them on and I took me real quiet down the steps to the cellar. That's a mean place at the bottom. I nearly fell through the door myself. When I heard visitors upstairs, I remembered what Nancy said about the cubby under the cellar stairs. You heard about that before, sir?'

Jack nodded.

'I crawled in that little closet. Wasn't much room for me, but it was a good place. 'At loud man come down the steps right past my door and never knew it was there. Then I heard him tumble and might' nigh bust his head open on that cement floor.' Louis grinned unsympathetically. 'But it just put his light out and sort of broke his spirit, I guess. He didn't nose around much after he got the candle lit again.'

'Do you want to sleep down there to-night?' asked Jack Fairfield.

'No-o,' Louis answered, 'I thinks I could sleep in a feather bed and rest fine the balance of the night. Seem like my mind's easy now. And iffen there ain't anything I can do, I guess I go upstairs now.'

He hesitated at the stair door. 'One thing more I'd like to find words to say. I 'spects I complained more than I should, Missy; I've had a hard time. But the kindness you folks showed me, it more than balances all the meanness I ever met. I — I wishes you didn't have to be hurt for me, Miss Susanna!'

'It will be all right, Louis,' Susanna assured him. Her head ached, and she winced as Jack knelt to adjust the tourniquet again, but she felt, too, a growing satisfaction; everything would be all right soon.

'Bleeding is nearly stopped,' Jack reported. 'It could have been worse.' He tried to choke back a cough.

'Jack ——' the girl said, 'I thank thee for being good.'

'Me? Good? I'll never be good like that again! To sit by while a girl runs all the risks!'

'But, Jack — they didn't find Louis. And the marshal has gone away. He says he won't hunt Louis any more. And I wasn't much hurt. They were a lot kinder to me than they would have been to thee. See, I can lift — my arm.'

'Don't!' the man said sharply. He took her cold fingers in his own big hand, and, under Tristram's astonished stare, he bent and laid his lips on them.

In that warm clasp Susanna left her hand; it was too painful to lift again, if she had wanted to, and she did not want to. Presently she raised her tired eyes to his handsome face, frowning in the low fire-light, and saw its stern lines soften.

'I'm not like that, my dear,' he said; 'but I can see that yours is a good way. I can even be glad I helped you play the game through this once. When you hear wild tales of me, remember this night, won't you?'

He broke off abruptly. 'That must be the doctor now. Tristram, don't you want to go to bed? We'll take care of your sister, and mend her as good as new!'

Some time later in the night, Susanna did not know just when, she found herself tucked away in the middle of the biggest bed the house possessed.

Her arm had been dressed and bandaged by good Dr. Way, physician to many an ill or injured escaping slave; her story had been told and discussed, with much speculation as to why the noise of the shot had not alarmed the sleeping town; it had been agreed that Louis could go on the next afternoon to Winchester without need of lying concealed for a time at Cabin Creek; and Dr. Way was quite certain that Susanna would not feel able to attend meeting in the morning.

Praises of Susanna's bravery and presence of mind had been thick about her modest head, and, when she was able to walk upstairs between the doctor and Jack Fairfield, she was commended again as an extraordinary patient.

Now the house was quiet at last; and Susanna lay staring at the shadows of the branches outside, flickering across the small window-panes. The moon looked in to see how far she had come on this adventure; Susanna wondered from what corners of the world she would yet see its friendly golden face.

In the dead stillness of the night she heard the sound of a horse passing slowly down the street. She struggled up painfully and saw, in the clear moonlight, Jack Fairfield riding by. He looked up at the house, but he rode steadily on to the southward.

Presently she slept, and in her dreams the throbbing of her arm was changed to the rhythm of a horse's feet, galloping faster and faster, farther and farther, into strange lands.

CHAPTER XVI

What Happened Afterward

FOLGER COFFIN possessed a writing-desk handed down to him by some Nantucket Captain Coffin, who had brought it home from his voyages in Eastern seas. When the desk was closed, it looked like an oblong box of some highly polished wood, with a brass keyhole in front; when it was unlocked, it could be opened and laid back, opened and laid back again, until, when it was completely unfolded, it covered all the top of a writing-table. And there was a secret drawer which only the owner knew.

When Susanna taught her first school, in Folger Coffin's neighborhood, she asked him to sell the desk to her, and he was glad to do it, since, as always, his luck had been bad and he needed the money. Susanna glued back the fine dark purple velvet lining where it had been scuffed loose from the fragrant sandalwood; she oiled and rubbed the satin-smooth wood, and she explored patiently until she found the secret drawer.

In this drawer she kept her most precious letters. After she had finished her evening's studying and had seen that Tristram had done all his examples in arithmetic, she liked to take them out and hold them in her hands. She knew them by heart so well that she did not always unfold them.

The first of them was written in Catherine Coffin's fine clear hand, addressed plainly to Susanna Coffin at Newport. It said:

MY DEAR SUSANNA,

John Fairfield came to our home last Second Day evening, bringing us our first direct news of thee. We were glad to know that thee reached Newport, but very sorry to learn of thy injury. I look for a letter soon to tell us how thee is recovering.

Levi and I believe it will be best for thee to stay in Indiana this winter, for more than one reason.

We hear that thee is generally suspected of assisting in a recent bold venture, but that no one knows what more experienced person may have been also involved. If thee returns to the city at this time thee can hardly avoid close questioning, and thee and the boy, as well as others, might be made to suffer for no good purpose. Feeling runs high; but I may say that it has not interrupted our own work.

There is another consideration. We should both like to see thee entered in the new boarding-school at Richmond this coming session. We believe thee would profit by schooling and think thee deserves the opportunity. We are well pleased with thee.

Levi has recently been entrusted with a sum of money which will provide for thy schooling for the

year, and he himself will add sufficient to support
thy brother. Thee may draw on our Coffin cousins
at the Richmond bank, as thee needs the money.

Frederika Rammelsberg asks me to express her
affectionate regards to thee, and to tell thee that
she plans to send thee a good winter dress of her
own making, and a box of cakes for the little boy,
when any one is passing.

I may tell thee that John Fairfield feels that he
has some responsibility for thy injuries and was
anxious to make recompense. I told him I believed
thee would prefer to accept gifts through thy own
relatives.

John is now off again. He would not tell me
where he intended to go, and I fear he will meet
trouble again, for he cannot be held. I gave him
medicine for his cough. I hope he will take it. For
all his wild ways he is a generous man and a brave
one. And he is a true friend of the slave.

With my love, I am

Thy sincere friend

CATHERINE COFFIN

The second letter carried a Canadian postmark.
It was very short.

DEAR MISS,

A kind friend is writing for me, to say that I have
reached Canada and found work. This leaves me

well and I hope that you and your brother **are** the same, and God bless you. So no more.

Respectfully

Louis X (his mark)

Catherine Coffin continued to write kind, sensible letters regularly to Susanna, though never again a letter important enough to be treasured, as the first one was; and Susanna heard once more from Louis, chiefly learning that he had married a wife who had taught him to read and write, and they were well and hoped she was the same; 'so no more,' all in his own laborious handwriting.

The third letter in the secret drawer came in an envelope that looked as if it had been carried next some one's skin for days before mailing. The small folded sheet within was closely covered with a bold, irregular writing. Letter and envelope alike were worn thin at the creases long before Susanna put them away in her sandalwood desk to keep.

The letter reached Susanna in the spring of her first year at boarding-school. It said:

DEAR MISS SUSANNA,

While I wait for the night to come I am writing to you. I hope you will not think I have been indifferent to your welfare because I did not write sooner. With all my heart I hope that your arm healed quickly and that you are passing a pleasant winter in school. *Do not, I beg of you, try any more dangerous journeys!* I have been engaged for the past few months in getting together a larger company than usual, under greater difficulties. The South is nervous and suspicious. It has not been wise to write anything by which I could be identified. As it is, I am obliged to take my company on to-night, a few days sooner than I had expected, because of a neighborhood rumor that the slaves are being armed to rise against their masters. I expect a fine run for it, like old times. Miss Susanna, I know you would not approve, but if you could see how glad these poor fellows are for even this slim chance of escape, you would not altogether blame me. I will tell you about them some time. It is growing dark, and I must make my way to our meeting-place. I shall give this to a trusted man to mail when he can. Let me sign myself only

Your friend

J. F.

Under the flourish of those two initials a neat laconic note was set weeks later by Levi Coffin, though unsigned:

At thy request I have made what inquiry I could. The plans of this company met disaster, but I have reason to think that we may see J. F. again in good time.